I0531101

cool
with
kenny **her**
wright

KW PUBLISHING

www.kennywriter.com

Cool With Her

Edited by Lucy V. Morgan
Cover design by Kenny Wright
Cover image © Aleshyn_Andrei/shutterstock.com

First digital edition electronically published by KW Publishing,
February 2014

First print edition published by KW Publishing, March 2014
Printed by CreateSpace, Charleston SC

Chapter 1:
Beer Pong

"If we win..." Amber tapped her red-painted nails on her red-painted lips as she thought. "You two kiss each other. Full on. Tongue and everything."

I blinked, glancing uneasily at Paul. We'd been friends since middle school, and while we were close, we weren't *that* close.

This wasn't exactly where I'd imagined my twenty-fifth birthday would lead: playing beer pong in the basement with my wife and three of our closest friends. It was *supposed* to be a huge party. A Quarter Century Party reminiscent of a high school coming-of-age movie. Instead, the forecast predicted snow and all but three bailed. Paul and Amber were two of the three.

Fortunately, getting drunk *was* part of the plan, and after more than two hours with the pony keg of microbrew, I considered it a rousing success.

"Alright, then," Paul said. His jaw set. That was not a good look for me. Amber knew how to play his stubborn streak against him and he'd taken the bait. "If we win. then you two'll treat us with the same. Fair?"

Paul stared across the table at Amber like this was high noon.

I glanced at Beth, who was studying Paul and Amber with amusement. When she looked at me and smiled, the image of Beth kissing Amber flashed through my mind. My pulse rose.

As always, my wife seemed to read my mind and was already rolling her eyes.

Keeping eye-contact, I grinned. "Seems fair to me."

"It's on," the competitive Amber said, her attention never wavering from Paul.

"Hold on, don't I get a say?" Beth asked.

Paul seized on the weakness. "See? Even your partner has doubts."

"I didn't say that—" Beth began.

Paul bowled on. "Amber, babe, you should listen to your friend and just give up."

The women exchanged a look. My wife gave a subtle nod and Amber turned back to us. "You know what? I'm so confident that we'll be watching you two gentlemen swap spit that I'll let you go first."

Again, my beer-soaked mind thought about our two tall, svelte partners in one another's arms. I picked up my ping-pong ball and lobbed it across the table, completely missing all the cups. Paul shot me a disapproving look before dropping back into a crouch and launching the ball into the center cup.

"Luck," Amber claimed, grabbing the cup and draining the beer it held.

Beer pong was simple enough. Ten cups, half filled with beer, were set up in a pyramid like bowling pins. Each team took turns trying to lob a ping pong ball into them, while the opposing team drank the cups that were sunk. Paul was good at it. I was terrible.

Especially with a distraction like Amber. When it became apparent that they were losing, she placed her hands on the table and leaned over my target. Her full breasts spilled out of the low-cut sweater.

"That's not going to work," Paul said. He licked his lips as his gaze lingered in her pale cleavage.

Unfortunately, it did. They evened up the score, 6-6. It wasn't time to panic yet. There was still enough game left for me to enjoy Amber's breasts and exchange funny looks with Beth.

Then the women pulled ahead and Paul called for a time out. "Are you into me or something?"

"What?" I asked.

"Do you want to make out with me?"

I blinked.

He went on. "Because you're playing like you do. You sank, what? One ball?"

"I'm sorry! I'm just not very good at—"

"I don't need that bullshit, Jace. I need you to step it up. Focus! Ignore Amber and focus, for fuck's sake!"

"Thanks, coach."

Paul was right. If I didn't start playing, I'd be kissing him. Amber and Beth were whispering conspiratorially to one another when I picked up my ping-pong ball. My wife giggled, looking over at me through her long lashes.

Amber didn't step away from Beth once I took aim. Instead, the women sidled closer to one another, nuzzling as they watched me shoot. My jaw unhinged a little as Amber curled her fingers along Beth's chin.

"You get your mind right?" Amber taunted.

"I did." And with that, I sank my ball. Swish. After playing without focus, our opponents had finally given me some. If we won, I'd be seeing a whole lot more of this kind of teasing

"Fuck!" Amber pouted, stomping away from Beth.

We were tied at 8-8, two cups remaining in front of both of us. The pressure was on. Beth stepped up and knocked out one of our remaining cups. Amber missed hers. "Fuck!"

This was it. Probably our last chance to win. Paul stepped up to take the first shot. Everyone fell silent. The sexy opponents looked on, leaning on one another for support now, rather than seduction.

With his neat hair and week-old beard, Paul looked like he'd just stepped off the set of a Budweiser commercial, so this image was fitting: tiger stance, white ping pong ball in hand, red Solo cups half-filled with beer. He aimed, he shot, he sank it. It was a thing of beauty.

Dejected, Amber scooped up the cup and drank the beer it held.

My turn to put this away. My turn to give myself the best birthday present I'd ever imagined. And if I missed...

I looked at my fuming friend—more specifically, I looked at his mouth. At the scruff on his chin and on his upper lip.

I didn't want to think about *if I missed*.

I planted my feet just as I'd watched Paul do with every shot. I lifted my elbow, lining it up with the cup. The room was still. My forearm moved like a dancing snake: back and forth, slow and steady. With a deep breath, I released the fluttering ping pong ball. It sailed.

Oh, how it sailed.

When I finally released my breath, the ball was floating in the golden drink, and Paul and I had won.

Stepping forward, Paul clapped his hand on my back. "Well done, birthday boy. Well *done*." Amber blinked at the ball like it had betrayed her. Beth shook her head at my grin, which stretched from ear to ear.

Beth turned to Amber. "You'd think he'd made the game winning goal for the Stanley Cup."

Amber still couldn't believe she'd been beaten. She wasn't a woman who liked losing—especially to her equally competitive boy-friend.

"Now," Paul said, rubbing his hands together. "Pay up, ladies!"

Amber gritted her teeth, turned to Beth, and kissed her. Soft and swift. I wasn't really expecting much, and watching Amber's red lipstick and Beth's lip gloss stick to one another would be a memory I'd hold onto forever, but Paul immediately protested.

"Now wait a minute. I believe the parameters of the bet were to kiss, *full on, tongue and everything*. That was neither full on, nor tongue, nor everything."

Amber set her jaw, prepared to argue back.

"It's what you agreed to," I interjected.

Beth just shook her head slowly and mouthed *You dick* at me.

Amber looked from me to Paul, then back at me. "Fine, since it's your birthday."

Paul began to object. I stopped him with a hand on his chest as Amber stepped up to Beth and collected my wife's head in her hands. This wasn't the time to set the record straight. It was the time to watch.

Beth settled her hands on Amber's slender hips, batted her eye-lashes at me one last time, and turned back to her friend. The ladies drew close. Their lips parted. I caught the flash of pink before they came together. I watched the slow, open-mouthed kiss in disbelief. Every few seconds, one of them would shift and I'd catch a glimpse of their tongues swirling.

Beth's fingers tightened on Amber's hips, her fists clutching at the cashmere sweater. She retreated a little, pulling her head back, her jaw slack. Amber followed her, dipping close. Her fingers curled through Beth's dark hair.

I was uncomfortably hard, and was pretty sure I wasn't the only one aroused. The women seemed lost in their girl-on-girl kiss, going well beyond their end of the bargain.

I was so lost in the kiss that I didn't hear the creak on the stairs and didn't see the fifth member of our party join us.

Amber and Beth broke apart, their chests rising and falling rapidly. Beth let out a nervous laugh, which was shared by Amber.

"Seems like I'm missing out on a few things," Casey said from the stairs. We all turned to Casey, who stood there with her eyebrows raised. "I didn't realize you guys were *that* close."

"No, it's not—" Amber said, blushing.

Beth spoke right over her. "It was a bet."

I glanced at my long-time friend, wondering what she thought of this whole situation. With her hands in her customary gray hoodie and her nerd-girl glasses framing her sharp blue eyes, she looked almost the same as she had back in high school. And like all those times back then, I couldn't read her at all.

"Beer pong's a crazy game," I said nervously. "You never know where it'll take you."

Amber was going for another drink. Beth just stood there with a silly smile on her face, chewing on her lower lip.

"I see that," Casey said with a quick smile of her own. "So anyway, you guys should probably check out what's happening outside. It's kind of insane."

Beth was the first to the top of the stairs.

"Holy shit. Guess the weather guys weren't making up this stuff after all."

What could barely be considered a flurry when we'd gone down into the basement was now a full on blizzard. The outdoor lights illuminated a sheet of fluttering white.

We all raced to our own window and peered out at the snow. I flipped on the rest of the exterior lights and looked out over the front yard. We had a long, tree-lined driveway that was normally lit up like an airport runway. With all the snow, I couldn't even see the beginning of it.

Chapter 2:
The Set-Up

Excited laughter and cheers filled the ground floor. I'd been so skeptical of anything more than a dusting—and so angry at my friends for not showing—that this was a complete surprise. Turned out, they had every right to be cautious.

"It was falling like that when I came up to make my phone call," Casey said. "Must have been falling for hours while we were down there."

"Crazy," Paul said, wiping the condensation from the pane.

"You know what I'm thinking, right?" Beth asked me.

A look at her, and I knew immediately. The other three weren't far behind. One moment, we had our faces pressed up against the frosted window panes, the next we were rushing for the closet and hauling on our winter coats.

It's funny how much a person's coat says about his or her personality. This lot was all over the place, from Paul's lined black leather jacket to Amber's off-white puffy down coat. Casey wore a black pea-coat with the hood of her gray sweatshirt pulled up. Beth and I were the most appropriately dressed with our ski jackets and snow boots.

We poured out into a hushed world, our voices swallowed in the powdery snow. When I stopped to listen, I heard nothing but the soft rustle where the icier bits touched down.

Beth held her arms out and looked up into the sky, which glowed brightly despite the late hour. "I love how peaceful snow is."

I tromped over to the cars. They already had a good six inches on them, and judging from the steady precipitation, it wasn't going to let up any time soon. The long driveway had taken on an ethereal quality. Closer now, I could see the lamps glowing under the blanket of white, casting a ghostly half-light on the trees above.

I was about to comment on it when I felt something cold and wet strike the back of my head. Turning in protest, I caught a second snowball right in my face. Looking up, I saw Beth laughing at me, crouched down and already forming a third ball.

"You!" The snowfall muted my shout. I retaliated, nailing Beth before she could get her ammunition out of her hand.

Beth shrieked and retreated, stumbling a little in the snow as I chased her down. I tackled her in a snow drift that had formed up against the side of the house. She looked particularly cute in her hat and scarf: her round face was bright red with the cold, and snowflakes were caught in her long, dark lashes. I touched her cheeks as she smiled brightly up at me. "I love you, sweetheart."

"I love you, too," she replied before we kissed. Despite the snow on all sides, this felt cozy. "I could stay like this forever."

I nuzzled her nose and nodded my agreement.

"I don't think our friends're going to get home tonight," she said.

I nodded again. "Good thing we live at *The Warner Estate*."

We'd moved out to the ex-urbs to buy a home we could grow into—although with just the two of us, it was big enough to earn the palatial nickname. At least now, we'd actually have a use for the three empty bedrooms (two of which were actually set up as such).

That was when the snowballs really started to fly. Naturally, they went after our prone bodies. Helpless targets were hard to resist in the minds of children, apparently. Beth giggled up at me. "Or maybe we'll just leave them out here."

"Maybe."

We hopped up and returned fire.

****

When we finally entered the house, Beth announced that we should all take showers while she fixed something for us to eat. I suddenly realized that all I'd had for sustenance since lunch was a handful of potato chips and beer. My stomach growled just to underline the point. By the time I'd finished showering and headed downstairs, the house was filled with the mouth-watering scent of herb-roasted chicken.

Beth had changed into a dry pair of yoga pants and a loose top, elongating her already slender body. I stopped just inside the door and stared as she went about stirring pots and dashing spices into pans.

This woman was my wife. I couldn't stop smiling at the thought—one I'd had many times in the last year.

"Hey, how long have you been standing there?" Beth asked when she saw me.

I shrugged.

She handed me a wooden spoon. "Stir this, Mr. Voyeur."

I felt myself flush at the nickname. A couple months back, I'd gotten drunk and admitted that I'd like to watch her masturbate. She'd done it, but had also teased me ever since. "I never should have said anything."

"Now where's the fun in that?"

I changed the subject, glancing down into the pot of darkly simmering liquid that I was stirring. "Mulled wine?"

Beth dropped sliced fruit into the steaming red. "I figured since Amber and Paul aren't driving home tonight, and Casey's staying with us, then why not?"

"Yeah." I pulled her close. "But I wish we were alone. This could be so romantic."

She was almost as tall as me, her slim frame fitting perfectly against me—head on my shoulder, her breasts padding the taper of my chest. I remembered the first time I held her like this. It was in that moment that I knew I wanted to make a life with her. If all else failed, we had this perfect hug.

"I got something for your birthday."

"Oh yeah? I thought the new iPad was my birthday present."

She pulled back enough so that I could see the mischief in her eyes. "This is something else." She whispered, "Something super sexy."

"Super sexy, huh? Not just regular sexy?"

Beth feigned seriousness for a moment before dissolving into a fit of giggles. "Definitely super."

"When do I get to open it?"

"Tonight," she kissed me softly on my jaw. "Although if you're good..." Another kiss, this one closer to my chin. "I might give you..." Corner of my mouth. "A sneak peak..."

Our lips met and parted. The kiss began as playful and ended serious. I turned her until she was against the counter and let my tongue swim in the darkness of her mouth. Her hands tangled in the nape of my neck as I pushed my knee between her legs. I covered her ass, feeling the slinky back of a g-sting.

"Is that the sneak peek?" I asked, my thumb tracing along to the point where the three straps met at a T.

"That's part of it. But really, it's more wrapping than present."

"Want to go to bed early tonight? I'm feeling kind of sleepy from all the beer," I said.

Beth laughed, touching my face. "If that's the case, maybe I need to go find Amber again."

My cock thundered to life. I whispered, "That was hot. Have you two ever…?"

Beth just smiled as I trailed off, not taking the bait. Another conversation for another time.

Someone cleared her throat from the doorway. Casey. "Seems like every time I walk into a room, I'm interrupting Beth kissing someone."

"She's a good kisser. Maybe you should try it some time," I said.

Casey flicked her eyes to Beth without answering immediately. She'd put her dark hair up in a messy bun, further enhancing that nerd-girl look. I wasn't fooled. I'd seen her dolled up at prom. I'd seen her let her hair down and throw it back. I'd always found Casey attractive, but we'd known each other so long that never thought of her that way.

"Maybe I should." Casey's tongue peeked out between her teeth before she broke out laughing. "Hey, Beth, where do you keep the towels? I'm going to grab my shower."

"Oh, linen closet's next to the bathroom. Middle of the hall." Beth slipped out of my arms. "Let me show you."

"No, no, don't worry about it. I can find it. Don't let me interrupt anything," Casey said. "Smells great, though. I love mulled wine."

We watched the petite brunette go and for a second, I thought of where she'd be in just a couple minutes: naked in the shower.

"She's pretty," Beth commented, picking up the spoon and going back to her soup.

I tensed. Beth wasn't a jealous person at all, but I still worried about what she thought of my close friendship with Casey.

"I guess," I said.

"Jason, you know your eyes were all over her ass just now, don't you?" At least she said it with a smile.

"I…fine, she's pretty. But you don't have to worry about anything."

"Oh, I'm not worried. I was just making a simple observation."

The kiss I'd just watched her share with Amber colored that statement, but I let it be. "I'm going to build a fire."

"Sounds great, honey. I'll finish up dinner."

****

I paused just inside our living room and looked around. Beth and I owned all of this. I still couldn't believe it, even after signing the mortgage a solid six months ago. We'd considering staying in the city with our friends—with Amber and Paul and all the rest—but our frugal minds couldn't get beyond how expensive it was to buy so close. Even the traditional DC suburbs were crazy over-priced. We went for the ex-urbs of Maryland, where the price tags seemed to fit the square footage a little more.

The living room was one of the things that really blew us away when we first walked in. The cathedral ceiling vaulted two stories, and one side was completely made up of window-panes. Despite the nightfall, the snow reflected the distant lights of the city, illuminating the empty forest that surrounded "Warner Estate."

A stone fireplace dominated the room, surrounded by a sectional that we never could have fit into our old apartment. Like most post-grad professionals in our mid-twenties, the place was furnished from Craigslist and Ikea, although Beth had added her own touches with funky cushions and a rug she'd brought back from her parents.

One day, we'd have "real" furniture, but right now, it was perfect.

As I began to start a fire, I realized that I was going to run into a problem when it needed to be refueled. While we had a small stack of split wood beside the fireplace, most of the wood was under a tarp by the shed. I glanced out the large windows into our backyard—at all that snow. Suddenly it felt like there was an ocean between me and the wood.

Sighing, I stood up, went back to the door, and began strapping on my snow gear once again. Outside felt a lot colder now that I had a chore to do. It took three trips to haul in enough wood to get us through the night. It was still snowing hard without signs of stopping, and a few more inches had accumulated since we'd come in.

I set the kindling on a bed of newspaper, positioned three logs perfectly across the top, and realized I had no matches. Quickly checking in the kitchen, Beth told me that she had a stash in the office upstairs and shooed me out.

As I climbed our grand staircase, I wondered where Paul and Amber were. I hadn't seen them since they'd showered, and in that time, I'd done the same, made out with my wife, carried firewood into the house, and set a fire.

As soon as I got to the top of the stairs, I got my answer. Even with the hiss coming from the bathroom, where Casey was showering away, the moaning from down the end of the hall was unmistakable. I should have turned around and given them privacy—that's what the polite guy in me would have done. But Beth didn't call me Mr. Voyeur for nothing. I had to look.

The running water helped cover any creaks I may have made as I tiptoed down the hall. Passing the shower, I could hear Casey's soft humming as she cleaned herself. An image began forming again of her small yet curvy body covered in suds, but a sharp moan drew me back to the guest bedroom, where Paul and Amber had set up.

They hadn't shut the door all the way, and Amber's steady gasps grew clearer as I approached. My heart raced. Her moans were throaty growls punctuated by short exclamations. "Yes! Ahhh, yess…"

The first thing I saw was Paul's very naked ass, pale and hard, pointed in my direction. Shifting my angle a little, I treated myself to a more pleasing view of a prone Amber, clawing at the bedsheets. Her legs were spread wide on either side of Paul and he held her narrow waist in his firm hands. She contorted back like a diving board being bounced on, her breasts and naked upper body falling into view.

I'd seen Amber naked before, years ago, and her body was still as exceptional as I'd remembered. She had a similar physique to Beth—lean and sinewy—only with fuller tits and pale, unblemished skin. Where Beth had a dusting of freckles across her perky chest, the blonde had skin like paper and pale nipples barely differentiated from the rest of her coloring.

"Fuck me, Paul! Ahh yes!!" The blonde was frantic. She arched back as Paul buoyed her up by the hips. She wrapped her long legs around his back and my eyes zeroed in on her anklet and the rings on her red-painted toes.

"So you and Jason?" he grunted, rutting into her harder and faster.

My ears perked up. I moved a fraction of an inch closer to the crack in the door.

"Yes, baby! Yes…ahhh…you feel so fucking good!"

"When?" His grinding hips demanded as much as his voice.

"In…ahhh…in college…"

My face grew hot. It was true—we'd dated very briefly back in college—but it was one of those relationships that burn fast and bright and die even quicker. I'd never told my wife, and apparently she'd never told Paul. Until now.

I started worrying that this would hurt our already competitive friendship. I wondered if Paul was going to storm out of this room and fight me. He'd always been the type not to back down from an argument—the guy who'd gotten into a physical fight over who was a better first round pick in the NFL draft last year.

So it came as a complete surprise when he said the next thing.

"God, that's hot." He never stopped his sadistic thrusting. "Have you done it since?"

"N—no..." Amber mewed, unable to concentrate.

"Have you thought about it?"

"Mmm...you'd like me to, wouldn't you?" She dug her heels into his back and writhed on the bed.

"Have you?" he demanded.

I found myself as close as I could get to the door jam without actually being in the room. I was all ears.

"Oh yeah, baby. He was good..."

I nearly came right there. I was floored.

The couple rolled together until it was Amber's naked back and buttocks I could see, along with a generous amount of side-breast. Paul reached up and cupped them as she eased into a galloping rut.

I had to shift my position a little to keep watching, but hell if I was going to leave now. Not with the tantalizing view of Amber's toned, naked shoulders and upper back, or the narrowness of her waist and the deep dimples that formed in her lower back.

"You thinking about him now?" Paul was actually getting off on this.

"Yes..." Amber raked her fingers through her thick hair.

I remembered how good she felt. Memories crashed home, along with guilt. I should have told Beth about us, no matter how short it was. I'd fooled myself into thinking that it hadn't meant a thing, and now all those memories were back.

"You close?" Amber huffed. Her gyrations were deep and quick.

"Yes," Paul groaned.

"I'm thinking about him now. I'm thinking about the birthday boy's thick cock fucking my pussy...filling me so good...filling me like my boyfriend's can't..."

"Ah, shit, baby!" Paul growled, grabbing Amber's head and yanking her lips against his.

Amber's moans were deep and sharp, each beginning to trail off before being buoyed by the next. She tossed her head back, her honey blond locks flowing down her back. Her orgasm mixed with Paul's. She collected her tits in her hands and squeezed, pinching her nipples.

I didn't realize that I'd begun to touch my erection through my jeans until my own cum nearly joined theirs. Fighting back from the brink, I faded away from the door and took a deep, steadying breath.

The couple's moans tapered to gasps and sighs. To swishing sheets and soft kisses. I found my composure. The silence in the hallway was thick. Casey had finished her shower.

Heat filled my face. My heart leapt into my throat. I turned and crept away as quickly as I could, disappearing into the office just as I heard Casey rattle open the bathroom door and step out. I held my breath. I watched the doorknob, waiting for Casey to burst in. I raced to formulate some explanation for why I'd been peeping into Amber and Paul's room.

Instead, I heard Casey's padded footsteps pass the door, pause by Amber and Paul's room, then continue on to her own.

I released my breath, found the matches in the drawer, and hurried back downstairs.

****

It was only as I watched the flames curling the newsprint black before hitting the kindling, that I got past that adrenaline rush of nearly being caught. The things I'd heard Paul say—that Amber had confessed—came racing back.

I'm thinking about him now.

I'm thinking about the birthday boy's thick cock fucking my pussy...

Filling me like my boyfriend's can't...

I never would have guessed that Paul had a cuckold fantasy. Not in a million fucking years. He was the guy who brought a six-pack of cheap American lager to every sporting event he attended. He was the guy with season tickets to the Redskins and took the day off on draft day to watch the team picks.

I'd known Paul since kindergarten, and he'd always been the cooler, tougher kid. I'd looked up to him, and for whatever reason, he'd kept me under his wing. Me. The fat kid. The total nerd. Girls who looked like Amber—leggy blondes who looked like models— saw me as a *friend* if they saw me at all. I was certainly not the object of their fantasies. My circle of friends amounted to Paul and Casey, and I'd never even felt up a girl until college.

College. That was a big shift for me—a clean break. I joined the wrestling team and lifted weights. Running became my religion. I traded fat for muscle, and insecurity for confidence. I joined a frat. I started dating.

Thing was, even as I shed the weight and hooked up with girls like Amber—including Amber—that stigma lingered. When I thought of myself, I didn't see the clean-shaven guy with the tumble of dark blonde hair—the guy Beth called distinguished and hand-some and all kinds of other things I felt too modest to admit even to myself. I saw the fat kid. The one who was laughed at when he asked Michelle Thompson to prom.

So how did that guy become the subject of Paul and Amber's

bedroom fantasies?

I couldn't stop the smile from forming, and since I was alone, I let it grow into a shit-eating grin. How fucking cool was that? Maybe I wasn't so insecure after all.

I let the heat of the fire wash over me. Paul's fantasy wasn't that unusual. Plenty of guys fantasized about their partners with other men. And who doesn't think about an ex-lover from time to time?

"Proud of yourself, aren't you?" Casey startled me out of my revelry. She pointed to the flames as they grew taller, twisting and flickering up the chimney. "Explain that one to me?"

Her question threw me off. For a second, I thought she was asking for my thoughts on being the subject of Paul and Amber's fantasy. When I realized she was asking about the fire, I sputtered to say something.

"Well, guys like, um...fire."

Turning to look at her, I saw that she only had a towel on. The towel didn't do much to hide her full breasts and the perfection of her skin, turned golden in the firelight. Her dark hair was still wet, loose and pushed back from her face.

Recalling what Beth had said earlier, I mentally corrected my wife. Casey was more than pretty.

She said, "Lost your train of thought?"

I shook my head, more to clear it than deny. "Sorry. Distracted."

Casey had a bright smile. "By me? Or by Amber and Paul upstairs?"

"So you heard that, too?"

Casey laughed. "I couldn't not hear it. They left their door open! Almost like they *wanted* to be heard."

Now that was something I hadn't considered. "Maybe."

"Could you do me a huge favor, Jace? I left my bag in your car when I arrived and as much as I'm flattered by your eyes all over me,

I'm going to get cold really soon. Mind grabbing that for me? You still have your boots on..."

"I don't know. I do like this look on you."

"Uh huh."

"Be right back."

Along with Paul, Casey was my kindred spirit when we were growing up. We were a clique of three, not really fitting into any one group. We were both studious, but didn't fall in with the geeks and nerds. We certainly weren't part of the popular kids, although Paul got us invited to a couple football parties in our senior year. Mostly, though, we were just a trio of teenagers, undefined by the social categories that television and movies tried to enforce.

I grabbed the suitcase from my SUV and vowed that this would be the last time I'd brave the snow tonight. It was my birthday, after all. Paul could do the chivalrous thing next time.

Casey met me at the door, shivering as she took her bag and ran upstairs to change. I checked in on Beth, asking her if she needed any help. She just handed me a glass of mulled wine and shooed me out.

Out in the living room again, I sat by the fire and drank my mulled wine. Casey joined me a few minutes later, mercifully dressed in a sweater and a pair of tight jeans.

"That's better," she said, taking a seat on the floor in front of me.

"Says you."

"Please, Jason. You're too much in love with Beth to be comfortable with half-naked women walking around you all the time."

I sipped my mulled wine, then changed the subject. "So you're dating someone now, I hear?"

A smile tugged at her lips. "We're still figuring it out. It's kind of...complicated."

"Oh?"

"He's a coworker, so there's that..." She looked like she was going to say more, but nothing emerged.

"Yeah, the whole workplace thing can be complicated."

"Oh, you have no idea." Casey took a sip from my glass of mulled wine without asking.

"But you're having fun? You like him?"

Holding the warm beverage with both hands, she nodded. "I'm having a ton of fun."

"Good. That's the most important thing."

"So how's married life? Has the honeymoon period worn off yet?"

I thought about the g-string that Beth had teased me with earlier and grinned. "We've only been married a year, but honestly, I can't imagine it ever wearing off."

"You two are good for each other," Casey said. "It's kind of inspirational to watch."

Before I could reply, Beth swept into the room carrying a collection of dinner plates. "Should I be jealous?" she asked.

I realized how close we were sitting, with me on the stone fireplace and Casey on the floor at my feet. Casey replied for us. "Trust me, Beth, you don't have to be jealous of this one at all. He's too in love with you."

Beth met my eyes. "Then he can help me bring the dinner out."

Chapter 3:
The Game

Paul and Amber finally joined us, walking down the stairs hand-in-hand. Casey and I shared a knowing glance as the couple settled in around the fire.

We decided to eat around the fireplace. The wine flowed along with the conversation as snow continued to pile up. Beth filled us in on how the DC Metropolitan Area can't handle snowstorms—not like they could in Colorado where she grew up. Paul made a misogynistic reference to her being a snow bunny and Amber pouted that *she* wanted to be the snow bunny.

"You would've loved the hot tub at my parents' house," said Beth. "It was perfect for days like this. Nothing like coming in from a full day of skiing and soaking in that thing."

We'd set our dinner plates aside and sat in a semi-circle around the fire. I was on the long piece of the sectional and Beth was on the floor at my feet. Sharing my fascination with pyrotechnics, Paul was parked next to the hearth, prodding the flames, while Amber and Casey shared the other couch.

"I could go for a nice soak right now," Amber said. She looked at me quickly, then back. "Did you ever get any action in there?"

That earned Amber one of Beth's eye-rolls-with-a-smile. "I've brought a boyfriend or two home while my parents were out..."

"Now there's something I'd like to try." Amber turned to Paul. "Honey, let's install a hot tub at home!"

"Sure thing, Amb," Paul said sarcastically. "We can have it built on the balcony, next to the fantasy herb garden we have out there." Amber and Paul lived in a condo in the center of the city.

"You're no fun. So tell me about it, Beth. Was it hard to do in the water?"

My wife shifted a little against my legs before answering. We never spoke much about our past experiences. We both knew we'd been with other people and were fine with leaving it at that. I'd never been too curious. I felt differently now. My ears perked up. I wanted to know.

"At first, yeah... I mean, things aren't as slippery underwater, you know?"

We'd had sex in the shower on a few occasions and she was right, it was never easy until you got started. Then it was incredible. I'd never thought about it, but Beth'd used a few tricks to get us started. Now I knew why.

"I bet."

"I never got that," Paul added. "I mean, if it's so hard, why bother?"

Casey smirked, like she had something to add. But as usual, she kept quiet.

Beth shook her head. "I don't really know. At the time, it felt like I was rebelling against my parents, so there's that. Plus, it just felt good, being surrounded by all that hot water while..." She glanced up at me. "Anyway, you two should try it sometime."

"Seeing a new side of your wife?" Amber asked.

I'd consumed too much mulled wine to be anything but honest. "This whole night's been...educational." *Paul with his cuckold fantasies. Beth's past sex life. The way Amber and Beth had kissed.*

"Educational *good*?"

"Yeah, I think so."

Beth eyed me like a poker player searching for a bluff. "If you want to know something, honey, all you have to do is ask."

I didn't know what to say to that. I eyed our audience, suddenly wishing that the three of them would go away. Paul spoke before I could form a thought, much less a response.

"Hold on, one sec. I want in on this, too."

Beth swiveled her head in my best friend's direction. There was a hint of challenge in my wife's normally calm voice. "Go ahead. I've got nothing to hide."

"How about we play a game?" Paul suggested. "Never Have I Ever..."

"Is everything you do so structured?" Beth asked. "Don't tell me you two have a scheduled sex night."

Amber burst out laughing.

Paul's chin jutted out. "You have a better idea, Mrs. Freebird?"

I was pretty sure Beth would be fine having no guidelines at all. I also had a hunch that Paul wanted more, and now that he'd been challenged, he wasn't going to back down until he got something. Personally, I was intrigued by where this was going, so I offered a compromise. "Okay, how about this. Someone asks a question, everyone answers. Simple enough?"

"I like it. There shouldn't be secrets between any of us," Beth said. Thinking about my history with Amber, I wasn't so sure about that.

"We all good with this?" I asked the group, but mostly it was directed at Casey. Amber, Paul, Beth, and I had always maintained a flirty relationship. We got together frequently—even before Beth and I got married—we drank too much, went out to clubs and swapped dance partners. Casey lived in Philly, and while I saw her more than a few times a year, usually, I still saw her as my high school friend. I felt the evening taking a turn and worried that things were about to get awkward for Case.

Instead, she stood and held up her empty glass. "I'm totally in. But first, let's get refills."

"Awesome," Amber said, joining her.

Paul stood as well. "I'm going to get another beer. Jace?"

The kegs were outside to keep them chilled. "Sure, but I'm not going out there again. Get me a refill?"

"Sure thing, bud."

Alone with Beth, I slipped down to the ground and hugged her. She had such beautiful eyes, large and dark. It was her eyes that I'd fallen in love with first. "I love you, Beth."

"Happy birthday, baby." She kissed me. When she pulled back, her brow was furrowed. "If you want to call it a night, we can."

"I'm good."

"You sure? We never talked about our pasts much," she said.

I pulled her closer, running my thumb along her soft cheeks. "I promise, I'm good. Those three are closer than family."

Beth giggled. "Good thing they're *not* family. I have a feeling we're going to be confessing things I'd rather not tell my brother."

"Ditto." My heart skipped. She was right. There was no way those questions were going to be PG.

The fire was getting low, so I went to work adding logs and poking it back to life.

Beth asked me the same question Casey had. "Both you and Paul seem to obsess over that fire. What's up with that?"

This time, I didn't have Casey's scantily clad body—and the

guilt of looking—to distract me.

"Something about creating something that's both beautiful and deadly, maybe? I don't know. I like it because it clears my mind. Like when you do yoga."

"My contemplative husband." Beth stroked my shoulder.

Paul returned with two Solo cups of beer, spilling them as he set them on our coffee table.

"We need to figure out a few more things," he said.

"How about you not staining our furniture, for starters?" Beth said.

"Oh, I see how it is. *Now* you have rules."

Beth tossed a napkin at Paul as Amber and Casey came in from the kitchen, armed with three full glasses of wine and an unopened bottle.

Paul pressed on. "So does the person asking the question need to answer?"

Beth took a seat next to him and wiped down the spill, even though Paul had already taken care of it. I laughed to myself as Paul's jaw tightened.

I got back to Paul's question. "Let's keep it up to the person asking. It's voluntary."

Paul's Type A personality objected, but he let it slide. "Fine."

"So we ready?" Beth asked.

Amber took a seat on the hearth opposite the fire from me. "Definitely."

Casey sank into the loveseat by herself, a glass of wine in her hands. "Me too."

Amber tossed out the first question, and it was directed right at me. "I want to know sex partners. How many? I know Paul's, and have a hunch on Beth's, but I'm clueless about you, big boy."

My body was warmed by more than just the fire. Like I said, this wasn't an area that Beth and I talked about much, and I was a little ashamed at how slutty I was back in college. I always justified it by my complete lack of action in high school, but that didn't make the number sound any better.

"Uh…" I glanced at Beth, who just batted her long lashes over at me. "Uh, I don't know. A lot?"

"What's a lot mean?" Amber asked. "Don't tell me you don't actually know…"

"Fine. 20."

Amber slid across the slate hearth of the fireplace until our hips touched. Her blue eyes were alight. "Paul, how many have you had, again?"

"19." He gritted his teeth.

"I'm sorry to hear that Jason is just a little bit more of a man than you," Amber said sweetly, resting her head on my shoulder.

Amber and Paul were back in competition mode. I wondered if they were like this when they were alone, then thought of the two of them upstairs and realized that they probably were.

Then Paul said the worst thing possible. "We'd be tied if I'd slept with your wife, too."

Here was the problem with goading Paul. He got vindictive and reached for the freshest weapon at his disposal: knowledge of me and Amber.

"What?" Beth swiveled around to look at Paul.

"Oh, your hubby didn't tell you about the two of them?"

"Really?" Beth turned to stare at me.

My body burned, and it wasn't just from the proximity to the fire. "It was a long time ago. Before we met."

I glanced at Paul, who was looking pleased with himself. I hoped he saw the murder in my eyes.

Beth reached out and took a sip of her mulled wine. I wasn't sure what she was thinking, but I was pretty sure it wasn't good. When she glanced at me and Amber, I realized how bad this looked. Like love birds in front of the fire.

Beth's bangs fell across her face as she slowly shook her head. "That explains a lot."

I glanced at Amber, who looked just as confused as I felt, then back at my wife. Beth was laughing.

"What?" I asked.

"You two are funny. You could have *told* me, you know. It's no big deal. Just...you guys always seemed closer than most platonic friendships, you know? Different than Casey and Jace." She turned to look at the diminutive brunette. "You're not one of the twenty, are you?"

Casey laughed. "Don't worry. Jason was too in love with Michelle Thompson to notice a nerdy girl like me."

"Let's not go down that road, please," I mumbled.

"So why didn't you tell me? Apparently, Amber told Paul."

"I should have, yeah. Just...never seemed like a good time. And then it was too late, you know?"

As I spoke, Beth set her glass of wine down and crawled into Paul's lap. Pin-pricks of jealousy tickled my scalp as she whispered into his ear. "Paul, maybe we should punish them. Get your number up to 20?"

My throat tightened. "Beth..."

"Hey, I'm game," Paul said. I knew they were joking around, but I didn't like the way his eyes lingered on Beth's body when she looked over at me. He'd stolen a girl or two from me before, and while things were now much different, I still didn't like it.

I looked over at Amber, who wasn't taking the situation nearly as seriously as I was. She just rolled her eyes and looked at Casey. "How about you, Case? Are you more or less experienced than these mansluts?"

A sly smile spread across Casey's face. "First of all, sheer quantity has nothing to do with being more or less experienced, believe me." Clear blue eyes shimmered behind her dark glasses. I wondered what secrets she held. I knew that she'd been pretty adventurous in college, but we weren't the type of friends to exchange sex stories.

Then, she added, "But I've also had more than either of them."

All attention was on her. "How much more?" Amber asked.

She squinted, as if thinking. "I hit 22 in Vegas." She took a sip of her wine. "But my number was only 19 before I went out there."

"Wow." Beth wiggled a little in Paul's lap, and I wondered what she felt there. "And here I thought my ten was pretty high."

After hearing all these numbers, her ten should have sounded low—*should* have, but didn't. I knew my wife was active before me, but not *ten guys* active. I did the quick math. We'd started dating toward the end of her sophomore year and had been exclusive ever since; she was nineteen. To have nine guys before me was something I couldn't wrap my head around.

I met Beth's eyes. She was smiling, but I could see the concern on her face. *I love you*, she mouthed. I mouthed it back, still feeling uncertain.

Amber blew out a sigh. "Well, that was enlightening."

"What about you? You going to answer?" Casey asked.

The blonde laughed. "I think I'm going to pass, but you guys are making me feel like a saint in this room."

Beth seemed more interested in Casey's number than not hearing Amber's. "So Vegas lived up to its name?"

"Oh yeah. You just have to go into it with the right mindset."

I cleared my head and focused on Paul. He still had a chatting Beth in his lap and I didn't like it. "Refill, man?" I asked, hoping to get him up.

He just held his cup out to me and grinned. "Sure, I'd love an-other."

Jealousy tickled up the back of my neck—especially since Beth didn't even seem to notice when he put his hand on her hip. I clenched my jaw and grabbed the Solo cup from him.

"Fine. Everyone else get your refills. When I'm back, I get the next question."

Chapter 4:
The Fantasies

The scene was close to the same when I got back. Beth had slid into a recliner on the sofa, but her feet were still propped in Paul's lap. Amber was still by the fire and Casey still on the loveseat. I thought about breaking up the Paul/Beth combo and sitting between them, but went right back to the fire.

I decided to go for a more insidious payback.

I locked eyes with Paul. "Tell me about a fantasy that you have, but I don't know about."

I saw the instant doubt flicker in his eyes. The worry. He was wondering if I knew something, if I knew of his little fantasy: that despite all that bravado he put on, deep down, he wanted to be cuckolded.

"Okay..." he said slowly. He pulled his eyes away from me, glanced at Amber briefly, then settled on my wife.

"Well played," Amber softy whispered, barely audible to my ear. Amber knew I knew? Interesting...

"A fantasy that I've never revealed to you," Paul repeated. At first, I thought he was stalling for time. Then I realized he was looking at Beth. "I know you were joking just now, but...but my fantasy's you. From the second Jason introduced me to you... He's a lucky man."

The room was silent but for the crackle and pop of the fire behind me. He wasn't bullshitting. Like the epiphany that must have hit Beth when she learned about me and Amber, suddenly, so many things made sense. The way his voice softened when talking just with her. The way he would watch her from across the room. So many little things...

And me? An ugly possessiveness seized me. Beth wasn't in his lap anymore, but all of a sudden, all those touches, hugs, and the seemingly innocent flirtations came thundering back. How innocent had they been? I saw green in the darkening living room.

"Well..." Beth said. Few things truly left her speechless. "Um..."

"So this is a little awkward," Casey added.

"That's not very funny, Paul," Amber said. I heard fire in her words.

Paul looked over at Amber, his face hardening. The growing shadows gave an edge to his beer commercial handsomeness—the Dude in him had a dark side. "Jason wanted to hear about a fantasy he didn't know. Judging from his reaction, he didn't know that one."

Amber went on. "And me? Were you going to tell me you've got the hots for my best friend?"

"Only if you got enough drinks in me and we played a party game."

Amber didn't even bother addressing Paul. She looked over at Beth. "I'm really sorry about this. We're having a bit of a...thing now. I don't know."

Beth glanced quickly at me, checking to see if I was okay, then did what I loved her for: she broke the ice with hardly any effort. "Well, that means I'm that much closer to my own secret fantasy. I've never been with two men."

I wanted to leap across the room and kiss her.

Then I realized what she'd just confessed and my jaw dropped.

"Oh, you should definitely try that," Casey added, further dispelling the heavy scene. "It can be intense, but so, so good."

All eyes turned on Casey now, who was cleaning her glasses with the bottom of her shirt. She looked up, set her dark frames back on, and pretended to see us there for the first time. "What?"

Beth spoke for us all. "You're full of surprises."

"Good. That's the way I like it." There was so much mischief in that smile.

To me, Beth said, "I'm starting to see why you like her."

Casey laughed. "Oh, Jace liked me 'cause I let him copy answers on tests."

"Not true!" I denied.

"Oh? You would have passed Granderson's pre-cal midterm without my help?"

"I was..." Shit, this whole time I thought I was getting away with something. "Fine, whatever. You're the smart one."

"And the sexy one," Casey added.

Amber got involved, this time with a barb at Paul, of course. "I thought that's the title Paul always claimed in your trio."

Casey and I responded as one. "He did." And everyone but Paul laughed.

Paul gritted his teeth. "Aren't we answering questions here? So Beth? That's really your fantasy? A threesome with two guys?"

When the focus shifted back to Beth, she blushed enough to see in the waning light. "That's one that Jason doesn't know about. Yeah. I have lots of fantasies."

Paul pressed, as intense as ever. "Any specific guys in mind?"

"Taylor Lautner and Zac Efron would be yummy."

Despite the flip response, she kept shooting me glances, checking that I was cool with it.

I was. Just surprised to learn something new about her. We were pretty open with each other about our fantasies, but she was right, I'd never heard this one. I thought of her shared kiss with Amber—and her nine past lovers—and wondered what other secrets she had.

Her blush deepened under my thoughtful stare.

She cleared her throat and looked at Casey. "So what about you, Case? Do you even have any fantasies left?"

Casey laughed good-naturedly. "God, Beth. You make me sound like a slut."

"I'm sorry. I didn't mean—"

"Don't worry about it. I probably was." She rolled her eyes. "Am? I don't know. College and the year after were definitely pretty crazy."

"Based on your 22, I'd say," Beth said, regarding my old friend in a new light. I'd always presented her as my nerdy high school friend and as innocent and naive as me, but despite looking pretty much the same, she'd apparently done a lot of *experiencing* in the past seven years.

"So a fantasy that I have that I haven't already fulfilled and Jason doesn't know about... Well, I've always wanted to go to Dubai."

We all laughed, even Paul, which was good to see.

"But I don't think that's what you're looking for, is it, Jace?"

"You can answer however you like. We're free to judge you if we think the answer's lame."

"Well, we wouldn't want that, would we? Okay, well, I've always wanted to watch a couple have sex."

"I'd definitely recommend it," I blurted. My clumsy attempt to be witty was entirely fueled by beer, and where Casey and Beth had managed to diffuse potential awkwardness with their revelations, mine added to it. And as if I was on a mission to make things as uncomfortable as possible for me, I turned to look at Amber as I said it. I looked away, but it was too late.

"So Mr. Voyeur had more experience than just with Beth?" Amber asked beside me.

"I may not have Casey's experience, but I've been around." I was so focused on being defensive that it took me a moment to process what she'd said: *Mr. Voyeur.*

I looked back at Beth. "You told her?"

At least Beth had the grace to look repentant. "Girl talk."

Paul came alive. "What are you three talking about?"

Casey looked just as interested.

Good, at least they hadn't told Paul.

Beth saved me. "It's not important. And it's Amber's turn to answer."

"Oh, this one's going to be good. Right, Paul?"

Paul looked at Amber sideways before realization dawned on him. "Amber…"

Amber ignored him. "For you to really understand, you need some background. Despite what you all probably think of me, I've always been a relationship girl."

"You've just had a lot of relationships," I said.

"I've had a few. But not as many as you probably think. I've never cheated on a lover. Never had a one night stand. Never woke up in a stranger's bed…" She paused. Paul fidgeted a little. "Thing is, I'd never been all that curious. I figured I could have most guys I was interested in, so why bother with that whole bar scene, you know?"

"At least you're modest," I said, nudging her hip.

"Hey, I'm being honest here! So anyway, a few months ago, Paul and I took a trip down to Cancun. We stayed at an all-inclusive resort—you know, drinks, meals, all of that came complimentary. It was paradise—literally. The only little hiccup was that Paul had to call in for a meeting on the second day. So I decided to go down and hang out by the pool bar. No sense in wasting the day listening to him drone on and on."

Paul was quiet, intently watching Amber spin this story. His hands were absent-mindedly rubbing Beth's feet, but he seemed more focused on Amber's story than my wife.

"It didn't take long for guys to start approaching me. Most of them were pretty ridiculous. Kind of the reason I never got into that scene. *Apart from being sexy, what else do you do?* That kind of stuff." Amber had a great laugh, especially when she was recalling something she really thought was funny. "Then Andrew came over. And he was hot." She locked eyes with Paul. "Since we were at the pool bar and everyone was in their bathing suits, it didn't leave much to the imagination. Dark hair. Broad shoulders. A little bit of a rough look to him. And best of all, he wasn't trying too hard. No pick-up lines, no obvious glances down my bikini. We ended up talking through several drinks."

The air in the room felt heavy. The darkness closed in as the fire began to die. If the lights went out, we'd be crushed in the velvety black.

"We flirted more as the minutes passed and the drinks were consumed. I lost track of time. When he excused himself to go to the restroom, I realized that I hadn't seen Paul yet. And I'd been out there for nearly an hour."

I glanced at Paul. His face was stony.

Amber continued. "Then I saw him. Sitting in a lounger at the other end of the pool, watching me over his book. I had no clue how long he'd been there, but I thought it was weird that he hadn't joined me, you know? But before I could go over and say anything, Andrew came back. Paul didn't seem to do a thing, so I went back to flirting." She took a sip of her mulled wine, now cold, and shook her head. "It

COOL WITH HER   **37**

was so fucking hot. Before I saw Paul, I was just passing the time, you know? But after that...after that I had an audience." She rolled her eyes and rubbed her thighs together. "God..."

"What happened?" Beth asked. Her voice barely carried over the popping fire.

"Not much. We flirted some more; Andrew told me that he had one more night at the resort and asked if I wanted to have dinner with him. You know, looking back, I know now that I actually did. But I was there with Paul, and I had no fucking clue what was going on in his head. We'd never talked about...others, you know? So I turned him down." She bit her lip. "Right after that, Paul took me back to the room and we had some of the best sex since I've ever had."

My breath came slow and heavy while my heart raced. The other three in her audience seemed similarly distant.

"So my fantasy is that I'd hooked up with Andrew in Cancun." She shook her head. "For the first time in my life, I wanted a one-night stand."

Beth was the first person to regain her speech. "Wow..."

"Yeah, I know, right? I still don't know what came over me that night. It just seemed so...so fucking illicit. With Paul right there, and this other guy running his hands up my knee."

I looked at the way her leg brushed up against me, slim and shapely through her tight jeans. Feeling a little alcohol-fueled bravado, I placed my fingers inside her knee. Her skin was hot beneath the thin denim. "Like this?"

Amber looked at me. "Yeah. Only a little...a little higher..."

She parted her thighs as I slowly glided my fingers up the inside of her leg. Her muscles rippled beneath my palm. "How high?"

"Higher," she whispered.

"Were you wearing a skirt?"

Amber bit her lip and nodded.

"Stockings?"

Again, a nod. "And garters. I don't like pantyhose."

Jesus, my brain rattled. "Did your Andrew find out?"

"Mmm hmm. My skirt was pretty short."

"I bet he liked that." My light caress stopped just at the inside of her tight thighs, where the lacy tops of her stockings would have been.

"You think?" Her laugh was soft. "Do you?"

Our eyes met again. I saw her the way I'd first seen her back in college: a nerdy kid's wet dream. I saw her the way I had when we'd dated so briefly. I'd been suppressing it ever since. She had wet, glossy lips and white, even teeth. I remembered how aggressive a kisser she was, and—

"You two need a room?" Beth asked.

The fire at our backs was almost gone, but I felt like I was burning up. Our audience watched from the shadows. Beth had an arm around Paul's shoulder and was whispering something into his ear.

Jealousy shot through me before I realized how absurd that was.

Paul nodded at whatever she said and together they stood.

"I think we should all head to bed. It's late..."

I couldn't read her expression. Was she mad? Was she hurt? Upset?

"Right. Bed," I said, rising with them.

Beth held up her hand. "Give me five minutes to get your *birthday present* ready. Then join me."

When she was gone, Amber sidled over to Paul and whispered, "Bet you wish you were Jason about now."

Casey shot me a knowing smile. "Good night, guys. I'm fucking envious of you all. I'm definitely not happy to be alone tonight."

The obvious joke was for me or Paul to invite her to join one of us, but the three of us had been platonic for so many years that neither of us went there, despite all the revelations of the evening.

"Night, Case," I said.

Paul added, "See you in the morning."

Left with just Amber and Paul—and more pointedly, very little of my buzz—things got awkward quickly. "Well..."

"Well..." Paul said back.

"Think it's been five minutes?" I asked.

"Close enough."

And I stumbled upstairs.

Chapter 5:
The Birthday Present

The bedroom lights were low when I entered. The Gypsy Kings played quietly—a sure sign that sex was imminent. Beth was lying in the center of the bed, stripped down to a red g-string and a wispy red baby doll. With that lustrous dark hair, long pale limbs, and yoga-toned body, I had to pinch myself. We'd been together five years, married one, and I still looked at her and wondered why she was with me.

And then I saw the item in her hand. Saw her drag it across the creamy expanse of her chest and down into her cleavage, where the baby doll was tied in a loopy bow.

"Hello, Mr. Voyeur," she said. "Nice of you to join us."

I didn't recognize the dildo, a clear shaft with a red and white helix swirling through the core.

"So your present to me is actually a new present for you, I see."

"What's yours is mine, right?" Beth spread her legs as she traced the dildo across her stomach. The g-string was thin enough that I could see the dark shadow of the landing strip perched above her pussy.

Beth gasped as she slipped the glass rod over her panties, her eyes fluttering shut. "I just pulled it out of the fridge. It's so...cold..."

I shut the door behind me. Then remembered to breathe.

"I've been thinking of this all night long, baby." She looked at me, heavy-lidded, and bit her lip as she pulled her panties to the side. Even in the dark, I could tell how wet the shaved lips of her pussy were. "I've been horny all night."

Beth gasped as she ran the cold tip of the dildo along her slit, careful to avoid her clit.

I leaned back against the door, mesmerized. I considered unzipping my pants, but didn't want to interrupt this scene. I shifted into voyeur mode.

Beth moaned as she grazed the chilled glass across her engorged button. "Mmm, after this, I'm going to be ready for a nice, warm cock."

Lifting her ass up off the mattress, she pulled off her g-string before going back to playing with herself. She circled her clit with her left hand—harder than I would ever feel comfortable doing to her—teasing herself with the icy phallus. Each time she did, a sharp moan punctuated her heavy breathing, and that urge to touch myself—to go to her—grew.

"You're so hot," I said.

She looked down at the seat of my pants. "Show me."

I peeled myself away from the door at last, crossing to the foot of the bed. Beth's stare never left me. Her fingers slowed to a languid play, but didn't stop.

Standing just a couple of feet away, the scent of her arousal was unmistakable. Closer, I could see her nipples through the flirty baby doll, perfect discs of pale caramel.

At last, I freed myself, all painfully confined seven inches of me.

Beth licked her lips. "That's going to feel so good."

I watched her zig-zag the chilled dildo down her bare lips one last time before pushing it inside her. "Uh, God!"

Ditto, I thought.

Beth drew in a quivering breath. She was close. I wrapped my hand around my cock, stroking it gingerly as I watched Beth withdraw the glass dildo. This close, I noticed the ridges spiraling up the shaft and the sculpted head like the cap of a real cock. When she stroked herself again, she didn't insert it. Instead, she rubbed the textured surface along her slit. She was so wet. So engorged. I was hypnotized as she picked up speed.

"Yes...yes..." She tried to stay quiet—tried to hold herself together. I loved that she couldn't. I loved the vixen that emerged. Her breath came in short bursts. Her nostrils flared. Her beautiful face tightened into a grimace as her orgasm blossomed.

And then she plunged the glass cock deep once again, angling those ridges hard against her clit. She bucked and bit down, but it was too late. She couldn't contain it any longer.

"Oh...oh yes!" Her climax tore through her. She rammed the dildo as far as it would go, arched her back up, and lost herself in the moment.

Her body eventually returned to bed—to Earth—settling into the soft mattress with a hefty sigh. The room materialized—the low light, the snow gathering in the window panes, the Spanish guitar on Beth's iPhone.

As I pulled off the rest of my clothes, I thought—not for the first time—about how hard it was to reconcile this wanton scene with the sweet version of Beth that I'd fallen in love with.

Despite the long legs, the large eyes, and flowing hair, Beth always felt real to me. Her beauty wasn't going to get in the way of being a truly down-to-earth person. She was a pre-med student not because she wanted the career or the money, but because she genuinely wanted to help people. She didn't volunteer at the nursing home just to put it on her resume, or organize fundraisers because she had to. That was all Beth, and it was one of the things that made me realize that she could be the real deal.

Yet beneath that, I discovered—am still discovering—this raw sexuality in her. The girl-next-door was far from a facade, but mixed in there was the kind of girl who enjoyed playing with herself in front of an audience, or made out with other women.

Or wanted a threesome with two guys.

Strangely, I didn't taste the acidic bite of jealousy that I was expecting. If anything, it made me hotter for the woman I loved. She had a nasty side, and that was awesome.

"You're so sexy," I whispered as I climbed onto her. She still hadn't fully recovered from her orgasm, but was lucid enough to wrap her arms around me when I kissed her.

"Happy birthday," she said weakly.

I rubbed my shaft along her slick pussy, just as I'd watched her do with her glass toy. She was cool on the outside, yet I could feel her heat radiating. I lined myself up, seeking that warmth.

"It's definitely been a *happy* birthday."

"Uh!" We groaned in unison as I filled her.

"Fuck, your cock feels like fire." Beth released a throaty laugh, waving the dildo between us. "We're going to have to use this thing again. Soon."

"How about now? You wanted a threesome."

She paused a moment, studying me carefully. I could practically read her thoughts, so I preempted them.

"I'm not upset. Or jealous. Just surprised. You never told me."

"You never asked," she said. She didn't sound defensive or argumentative—she was merely stating fact.

I thought about how much different this conversation would

have gone for Amber and Paul.

I fucked her slowly, adding my heat to hers as the Spanish guitars harmonized around us.

"Fair enough," I said at last. "We never talked much about our pasts."

Beth rested her hand on the back of my neck and pulled me close enough to kiss. "Because they are our *pasts*."

And that was Beth in a nutshell: light-hearted, unabashed, and honest. And then there was a hint of that vixen when she added, "But if you want to know something, just ask. I've got nothing to hide."

"Of your lovers, were they all guys?" I didn't know why I latched onto that question, but based on the way my cock surged inside Beth, I was okay with it.

"No." She tried to keep a straight face, but her smile bled through.

My heart skipped a beat. "How many were girls?"

"Mmm..." She rolled her eyes to the ceiling in thought. "Three. And yes, they were all hot."

Jesus. How was I learning this for the first time in five years?

"Was one of them Amber?"

Beth's smile was as mysterious as one of Casey's. "Are you asking me if I've kissed Amber before today? Of course. She was my Tri Delt big sis."

"Did you do more?"

"Are you asking if you're not the only Warner to fuck Amber?" She squeezed me with her legs. "God, you're hard."

"Did you?"

"Sorry to say, but no. We came close, but no, she's not one of the three." She drew me against her shoulder, bringing her lips against my ears. "You like that idea? Of me and my best friend getting all sweaty under the sheets?"

I nearly lost it. It took all concentration to stave off orgasm.

"Yes, you like that idea." She laughed.

"I'm afraid I can't lie. Not in this position."

"Oh?" She sank back into the pillow and looked up at me. "Can't lie, huh?"

Uh oh.

"Do you ever think about Amber when you're with me?"

"No." It was a knee jerk answer, but an honest one. Mostly.

She put pressure on my lower back with her heel, pushing me into her. "Really? Never? She's a sexy blonde."

"I love you, honey."

She laughed. "We're not talking about love, baby."

"You ever think about Paul?" I thought I was being clever. Instead...

Beth immediately answered. "Yes, of course. He's a sexy guy, in a golden boy, All-American way." She squeezed me close. "A lot like Amber."

"So his fantasy? You wouldn't mind fulfilling it?"

My question sent a surge of something hot searing through my blood stream.

Beth tickled the hairs on the back of my neck. "Only if you share Paul's other fantasy."

His desire to watch Amber fuck another man.

"Oh, Jace. You grew. You don't, do you?"

That was a complicated question, although until tonight, I'd never even considered it.

"I guess I understand it..." I said slowly. Understanding it didn't make it my fantasy, though, but I also didn't feel jealousy about it. If anything, the idea was pretty hot.

"Well, it definitely turned *me* on," Beth confessed.

"You mean Amber's fantasy? About being picked up by the

pool? That could be fun to try sometime..."

"Yeah, that sounded pretty exciting..." She squeezed me, urging me to pick up the pace of our slow fuck. "But that's not what I'm talking about."

I pumped my hips faster, tensing for a new revelation.

"What really turns me on is thinking about watching you and Amber..."

"What?"

"Mmm, just thinking about you two is..." Her eyes fluttered shut. She tipped her head back. Was she for real? "Fuck me, Jason. Fuck me like you'd fuck Amber."

I pushed up on my arms, putting enough distance between the two of us that I could look down at my wife. Study her. She still wore the baby doll; it clung to her tits with our sweat. She collected her swells in her hands, seeking out her hard nipples through the thin red. Her brow was tight, her face tighter still. And behind her eyelids, she must have been imagining me with Amber. Must have.

"Oh, fuck me, Jace. Fuck me like you did in college." Her legs tightened around me. "I *need* it."

"Like this?" I dug in, driving my hips harder than I normally did with Beth. "Amber liked it hard."

"God, Jace...that's so...uhh..."

I smothered her beneath me. Her skin was clammy and hot. I could feel her heart race, her breath scratch in her throat.

With my mouth right up against her ear, I whispered, "You feel so good, Amber. So tight. Just like I remember."

"Oh, fuck me. Fuck me, Jason. Come for me."

I kissed her neck and buried my face in her long hair. My balls tightened. I drove my hips faster, consumed by the shuddering stretch of her body beneath and the tight grasp between her legs.

In that split second before release, I imagined Amber there, taking it. Begging for it. Testosterone fueled those last desperate moments. I took her wildly, desperately, riding the ragged edge.

With one last drive of my hips, I released all that I had, emptying my balls deep inside Amber—Beth. Fuck. Fuck!

****

Beth stripped out of her lingerie and we snuggled beneath the comforter. We listened to the snow falling quietly outside before either of us spoke.

"So I take it you're not mad?" Beth asked.

"Mad that you have a fantasy of watching me have sex with a hot blonde?" I laughed, although more than a little of it was forced. "Um, no."

"Fair enough. You *are* a manslut."

"Hey now." I hugged her close. "Sorry I never told you about me and Amber. I guess you're not upset about that?"

Beth shifted so she could look up at me. "I think it's a pretty sexy image, but that doesn't mean I'm not upset. At least part of me."

"Oh."

"You could have told me. Should have. She's my friend."

"I wanted to—was going to. But..."

"You were scared that I'd be mad? Seriously, does that sound like me?" she asked.

"Guess not."

"I don't care what you did in the past. Like I said, it's the *past*. I'm more upset that you didn't tell me, is all." She smiled up. Apparently she wasn't all that upset. "Have you slept with any of my other friends?"

"None that you still hang out with?"

"Interesting answer. Who was she?"

"Morgan McDonald."

"My roommate?" She looked impressed.

"You're not angry, are you?"

"As long as it happened before we got together."

"It did."

Beth kissed my chest. "Guess we *have* shared a lover then."

"You and Morgan?"

"Hey, she was a hot brunette who liked to study in her thong."

"Really?!"

"No, but that's what you guys think the sororities are all like, right?"

"Tease. So you and Amber never hooked up?"

Beth rolled her eyes. "We're not like bisexual nymphomaniacs or something."

"You're not?"

"You're such a guy. I've experimented with three other girls, two of which involved a lot of alcohol. It was a phase."

"So you're not attracted to Amber?"

Beth rolled her eyes, but didn't answer immediately.

"Uh huh," I said.

Beth swatted my chest lightly. "Keep dreaming."

"Don't worry, that's the plan."

"What about you? You never shared your fantasy," she said.

"You know all my fantasies."

She twisted my nipple. "Don't be a smart ass. Tell me one that I don't know about."

I thought through my catalog of fantasies, but couldn't think of something that qualified. "You know mine. They're all standard guy ones: two girls, public sex, that kind of stuff."

"So you don't share Paul's fantasy?"

"You with another man?" The question alone triggered something, but I'm not sure it was all positive. "If you'd have asked me before today, I would have said *no way*."

"And now?"

"I don't know. You want that?" I hadn't felt this much uncertainty in a while. It reminded me of high school.

"Like I said, I think Paul's good looking, and I'd be lying if I told you that I haven't thought about it, but I'd never do something unless you were on board."

I thought about someone's statement from earlier in the evening. *Learning something new about your wife?* More like, *learning something new about myself.*

"You know what's actually really sexy?" I said.

"What's that?"

"You."

"Pretty sure you've got to say that."

"No. I mean, yes, you've always been sexy. But I like this other side of you. This naughty side."

"Is it so new?" The hand on my chest slipped down to cup my cock. "Remember when we had sex just before my graduation, and I wore nothing but stockings under my gown? I could feel you leaking out of me that whole walk across the stage."

"Yeah."

"Or how I let you film me playing with myself in the shower last month?"

"Okay, sure. I guess I just...all that stuff happened with me. I never thought about you doing stuff with other guys, you know?" My cock grew in her hand.

"Back to the past. Maybe you share more of Paul's fantasy than you think."

"Maybe."

"Happy birthday, Jason. I'm sorry that the snow scared everyone off."

"It's okay. This has already turned out to be one of the most memorable birthdays I've had." I looked outside one last time. "And I suspect that it's only the beginning."

Chapter 6:
Beth's Plan

My dreams were filled with fleeting impressions of sweat-covered skin, twisting and sliding in the dark. I'd catch glimpses of the details before they slithered away: Amber and Beth kissing, this time naked; Beth standing in the doorway as I fucked Casey, much to my shock; and most startling of all, me watching my wife wrap her lips around Paul's cock.

That last one came on like a freight train, horn blaring, destroying everything in its path. It was so visceral. I could practically feel what he felt—feel Beth's warm mouth do to him what she'd done to me dozens of times.

"Oh, Beth, baby. That feels so good," Paul groaned.

Or was it me?

I blinked, and she was between my legs, attacking my cock with her small mouth. I blinked again and it was morning. And Beth was still there, her dark hair bouncing with each stroke.

"Oh, Beth…"

She slurped off me. "Good morning, sleepy head. It's a little late, but I realized I forgot to give you your birthday BJ."

"Better late than never—ugh!"

I passed into the back of her throat and shuddered. Christ, she was good. She'd perfected her technique over the years, but she was no novice when we started dating. How many guys had she done this to before? She'd slept with seven of them, but how many others just got off with a quick suck?

I think I grew a full inch just thinking about it.

"Mmm..." Beth pulled off again. "What was that? Thinking about Amber?"

"What?"

"You jumped in my throat."

I reached down and brushed her dark hair away from her eyes. "No, not Amber."

Did she believe me? "You *know* you can think about her all you want, right?" She sucked on my crown for a moment. "I'm pretty sure I'm better, anyway..."

With that, she went back to work. She propped up my cock and plunged down on it. I hit the back of her throat again a couple times as she got used to the vigorous motion. Then I passed through the tight portal.

"Fuuuck..." I groaned, resting back on my arms. They felt stiff. Weak. Her tongue tattooed magic with each dive, swirling and playing with the sensitive underbelly of my hard flesh.

On her knees and balanced with her right hand on my cock, she'd let her left drift down between her legs. I loved it when she played with herself—the girl definitely loved giving oral sex as much as receiving.

She sucked harder, timing her bobs with her plunging fingers. "I'm close, baby, so... close..." I touched her shoulder. She didn't ease up—either on me or on herself.

"Mmmph...mmphh!" Each muffled groan was ecstasy around

my shaft. Saliva bathed my balls as her right hand got into the mix. Her fingers tightened and began jerking the loose flesh with each pump.

Had she ever thought of doing this with anyone I knew? With Paul? The shadow of my dream flittered back, swift and potent.

"Beth... babe... I'm... ah—AHH!" I erupted down her throat. Fluidly, she pulled back until she held just my throbbing cock head between her lips. Both hands went to the shaft, milking every last drop of salty come from my balls.

When she sat back, she was breathing just as hard as I was. "So, whose mouth were you coming in?" Beth asked as she eased herself against my side.

"Yours."

"Uh huh..."

"Seriously!"

"You're a bad liar."

"Fine. I...I was thinking about you and Paul."

Beth looked surprised. "Really?"

My cheeks warmed. "At the end there, yeah." That sounded bad, so I added: "I'd been dreaming it."

Okay, that sounded worse.

"Very interesting." She looked up at me, something else on the tip of her tongue.

"What?"

Beth shook her head. "Just the start of an idea. I'm going to grab a shower. Make me some coffee?"

I watched her climb out of bed, drinking in her nudity. I lay there for the longest time, staring at the ceiling and trying to gather my own thoughts. Beth was well into her shower when I finally dragged myself out of bed and went in search of coffee.

****

I entered the kitchen accompanied by the smell of fresh coffee and the sounds of the local public radio station.

"Paul, how about this one?" Seemed odd hearing Amber's thick voice so early in the morning. "Four letters. 'German-based car manufacturer.' Second letter is U."

"*Audi.*"

"Duh. Thanks."

The scene I walked into was disarmingly domestic. Paul and Amber were seated at our kitchen table, both absorbed in different parts of yesterday's newspaper. Casey was preparing omelets.

"Oh, hey there, sleepy-head." Casey beamed. "Want one?"

My stomach grumbled. "I'd love one. Thanks."

"You two took your sweet time getting up," Amber said. "It's almost eleven!"

The thing about the blonde was that she always looked put together. Even with her unwashed hair in a utilitarian ponytail, she looked like she could stand up, throw on some designer dress, and walk a runway.

That was a little of a surprise. I never slept in. Never thought I could. And it had felt much earlier than that. She looked back at the crossword puzzle. "Ha. How appropriate. Eight letters starting with a *B-L* and ending with a *D. A deluge.*"

I shook my head. I was terrible at crosswords and had no clue what seemed so obvious.

Casey answered for me. "*Blizzard.*"

Amber nodded, shooting me a *you're silly* look with her eyes and penciled in the answer.

"They're calling this the Snowpocalypse," Paul said, setting the front page down. "On the radio. Pretty stupid if you ask me."

"I think it's clever," Amber disagreed, just as I was about to do the same.

Beth joined us at that moment, looking fresh from the shower. She said, "See, this is what happens when you Easterners make a big deal about every little snowfall. When something significant happens, it's the end of the world in Biblical fashion."

"There's two feet of snow out there," Paul whined. "And it's still going."

"Whatever. This is a dusting." Now Beth was just being contrary. Even in Colorado, I knew this was a lot of snow for her.

Paul, naturally, didn't back down. "Well, if this isn't such a big deal, then you can go dig my car out and get my laptop bag."

"Absolutely!" Beth agreed. I didn't like that smile she was sporting, and I *really* didn't like the way she looked directly at me. "Jace, dear, can you go get Paul his laptop bag?"

The room burst out into laughter, although no one seemed to take notice that I wasn't contributing. "Coffee first."

****

Both radio and television were reporting this as the snowstorm of the decade, with accumulations of up to three feet. Snow would continue into the afternoon or early evening before tapering off.

We had plenty of food to last the five of us, not to mention beer— but I was thankful that more hadn't come to my birthday party. That could have been an ugly scene.

Amber and Beth were the same size, so Beth's wardrobe was open to Amber. Paul was a little bigger than me, but still squeezed into my baggier clothes. And Casey had traveled down from Philly, intending to stay the weekend, so had clothes through the next couple days. Coffee in hand and breakfast in our bellies, I started getting excited about the prospect of being snowed in with my closest friends.

After breakfast, we went back outside and continued our impromptu snowball fight. This time, however, we pulled down our ski clothes and properly outfitted our guests.

Things between me and Paul still felt a little tense. I caught him looking at Beth a couple times, which didn't sit too well with me after his fantasy confession last night. He told Beth about Amber and I felt like he'd broken some kind of code, whether she was upset or not. He received more than his fair share of snowballs, and being the kind of guy he was, he didn't back down.

At one point, I looked up just in time to see what could only be described as a snow boulder headed right for my face. I fell flat on my ass, leveled, cold, and angry. I heard Paul's laughter, and even before I'd fully recovered, I was on my feet, shooting for his knees. I was back in college, in the wrestling circle. I tackled him into a snowbank formed by our cars. His guard was up quicker than I'd anticipated, and before we knew it, we were rolling for dominance in the snow.

The women had to pull us off one another, although not before he'd torn my jacket open and shoved a handful of snow down my shirt.

"What the fuck is wrong with you?!" he shouted as Amber and Casey yanked him away.

The blood rage left me as quickly as it had come and I didn't have an answer for him. "You're an asshole," I muttered and headed for the house.

I decided to brood and withdraw, which was my usual coping method when I was upset. Paul receded into his childish *ignore* mode, pulling out his laptop (that I had retrieved!) and planting himself on the sectional next to the fire.

"Let this one blow over, right?" Beth asked Casey, who'd known me and Paul the longest.

Casey shrugged. "Usually works "

My wife agreed and announced that she was going to do a little house-keeping—an obsession she'd developed and I encouraged. "Want to play some Halo?" I asked Amber.

"Do you have to ask?"

Amber lived one floor up in my dorm Freshman year, and my first impression of her was that of a princess. She was exactly the kind of chick that I would have been intimidated to talk to in high school. So naturally, I forced myself to become her friend. I still remember how surprised I was to learn that—while she *was* a princess—she also loved video games. First-person shooters in particular. It was like one of those rare epiphanies in life that, in an instant, can change everything. I stopped making assumptions about people, and I stopped getting intimidated by anyone, no matter how attractive.

It marked the advent of my confidence. The New Me was born.

I let Amber lead the way through the living room and into the den. I could feel Paul's gaze on us and made an exaggerated show of checking his girlfriend out. Or maybe I used him as an excuse to run my eyes over her slim curves. She'd borrowed a pair of Beth's red cheerleader shorts that barely covered her buttocks, and I highly suspected that she wasn't wearing much under the yoga sweater that kept falling off her bare shoulder.

She looked over her shoulder at me, her long, golden ponytail whipping about. I drew my eyes off her ass just a little too slowly. She noticed, but didn't say anything.

"I get player one."

"Sure."

Here was the problem with Amber: she played video games like she played her relationships. She always needed to be the one in control, calling the shots. I could only take so much bossing around—

like most guys, which is one reason she went through so many of them—and she quickly grew bored of the submissive men who did. It took a rare man like Paul to both challenge and put up with her, and as much as I thought he was an ass right now, he was a saint for that.

"Jace, cover the right, I'll—no, higher! That hill!" Even playing in a cooperative campaign as allies, it never felt like much cooperation was going on when playing with Amber. "Jason, listen to me!" she barked once we'd died for the third time. We were playing it on hardcore mode and I was beginning to regret that. "In order for this to work, I need to draw them out, and you need to snipe them off when they're in the open."

We tried again, and begrudgingly, her tactic worked. I almost messed it up on purpose, just so I wouldn't have to face that smug smile, but it felt like that was something Paul would do, and I wasn't about to sink to his levels.

When she excused herself for a bathroom and drink break, I quickly set the difficulty to an easier mode that we'd be able to trounce. We were supposed to be relaxing, not getting all worked up.

She picked up on it right away, but didn't say anything about it. Instead, she used the slower pace to talk about other things.

"So did you enjoy watching us yesterday?"

I colored, thankful to have the game to focus on rather than the blonde sitting next to me. "I...shouldn't have watched. I didn't see much."

I caught her frown out of the corner of my eye. "Don't be embarrassed, Jason. How long have we known each other? Seven years?"

"Something like that," I mumbled.

"And I know you heard what Paul and I were talking about."

"Amber..."

"How does it feel to be the object of our fantasy?"

"Amber—"

"Take it from me, as someone who's had a lot of experience with that—being someone's fantasy, I mean. Enjoy it."

"That's what I love about you, Amb—your modesty."

"I thought you loved my ass. Or was it my legs? Or am I remembering that wrong?"

"Hey you two." Beth's voice snuck up behind us. I jumped. Amber seemed unfazed. "I don't need to be worried about this, do I?"

Turning, I caught her regarding us with her hands on her hips and a smirk on her face.

"Nope," Amber said. "Want to join us?"

Beth sank onto the couch on the other side of me and made a face. "I don't do video games."

Amber and I plunged on into our virtual world. Beth pulled out her knitting set and busied herself as we played. For a little while, I thought she wasn't going to say anything. Then, without looking up, she said, "So Amber, your fantasy's not just about having a one-night-stand, but having one with my husband?"

Amber laughed. "Nah. That's a totally different fantasy."

"Good to know," Beth said. "Remember when I just asked if I should be worried about this?"

"Beth, I'm not sure that I've ever even seen you worried. About anything. You're like the most easy-going person I've ever met."

"Fine, fine. Just make sure I'm there if something does go down," Beth said.

"Hey, you realize I'm sitting right here, don't you?" I said.

Amber ignored me. "Oh, you know how much I like being watched."

"I do. I know *very* well."

The blonde laughed, glancing across me at my wife. "I seem to recall that you have a little exhibitionist streak in you, as well."

"Okay, ladies, want to fill me in on what the hell you're talking about?"

The sofa creaked. Beth set her knitting down and turned to me, steadying herself on my thigh. "What do you think, Amb? Should we tell him?"

I noticed Amber's shots were a little inaccurate in the game, her focus a little bit off. "I'd rather *show* him...later..."

Beth giggled. "Could be a fantasy come true for Casey."

She returned to her knitting. I got up. "I'm taking a shower. You two can keep talking in your little code."

****

On the way up, I wondered what was in store for this bunch. Clearly we were all sexually charged. Beyond the obvious history that Amber and I shared, Beth and I had been pretty flirty with the other couple since we'd all gotten together, and Casey didn't seem fazed by it. We'd always toed the line, however, and I didn't think that would change tonight because of Casey. She had a guy back home. She'd keep us on the straight and narrow.

Or so I thought.

"Yeah, they're all good looking," I heard Casey say from her room. "Yeah, it's *those* two guys. And Jason's still totally hot... Mmm hmm. That make you jealous?"

Casey laughed at whatever was said on the other line, sharp and clear. "Well, I'm not sure I can get any pics, but I may have stories..." Another laugh. "You're so silly. I'm not the one stuck in a hotel with the boss. She working you hard...? Yeah, I'm sure you're really broken up about that..."

I crept by the door, leaving Casey to catch up with her boyfriend. Just as I was about to leave her earshot, though, I heard something to give me pause.

"Have fun, Adam. Give Linn a nice, hard fucking for me. Bye."

In the shower, I didn't know what the fuck to focus on. Casey's open relationship? Paul's desire to be cuckolded by me? Whatever the hell Beth and Amber were talking about?

So I focused on washing away the remaining cobwebs of last night. We were all adults here, and we all cared for one another. Things had a way of working themselves out—especially when those things involved my wife.

I took my time getting dressed. Beth had given me a new selection of boxer-briefs and I pulled on the red ones that she seemed to like so much. I regarded myself in the mirror. For a moment, I saw the old me in that mirror—flabby and shy.

"No, man. Stop doing that," I said aloud. Blinking it away, I saw who I was now. Cut. Hard-muscled and broad shouldered. I worked hard for this body, but it had always been a personal goal. I lost the weight for me. I toned up to live a more active life, to do things that I'd always wanted to do but was too out of shape to do.

To be at the center of another couple's sexual fantasy? I hadn't signed up for that, but I had to admit it stroked my ego. To hear one of my closest female friends tell her boyfriend that I was *totally hot*? To hear my own wife express that she'd like to watch me satisfy her best friend? These were all new things to me, and while it had been seven years since I'd transformed myself physically, that skeptical highschooler had a way of coming out.

I pulled on a tight black t-shirt to go with my jeans. Even considered going down there like this, short sleeves straining around my biceps, just to remind myself who I was. In the end, though, I grabbed a zip-up sweater for warmth and headed downstairs.

Beth and Amber were still in the den, doing what they were doing when I'd left them—although now they were talking about how to sell crafts on Etsy. I left them alone and went looking for Paul. It was time to clear the air between us.

I heard him in the kitchen and was about to push in when I heard him say, "You can't tell Jason."

I was tired of eavesdropping on everyone, but with a line like that, how was I going to resist?

"Oh, come on, Paul." Casey speaking. "He's been your best friend forever. He'll understand."

"It's pretty fucked up though, isn't it? Ever since I learned that he and Amber hooked up, I can't get it out of my head. What does that make me? A wimp? A cuckold?"

"Please," Casey said. "I know one of those guys. Trust me, you're not him."

Paul barked a laugh. "Your new boyfriend likes seeing you get taken care of by real men?"

"Jesus, Paul, you just can't help yourself, can you?" Only Casey would have been able to shrug it off. "No, I'm not talking about my new boyfriend, but Adam and I do have an understanding about that stuff. Point is, you just want to see Amber in action, right? She's a hottie, I don't blame you. You're more like me—it's fun to watch a partner just go for it. For a...*cuckold*, I guess, it's more about him. He gets off on being marginalized. There's a humiliation aspect to it, you know?"

"Right," Paul said.

I thought about what I'd overheard yesterday in the bedroom. Amber saying: *I'm thinking about him now. I'm thinking about the birthday boy's thick cock fucking my pussy... Filling me like my husband's can't...*

Huh.

I backed away, going back to the women. At least arts and crafts was a relatively normal topic of conversation.

****

Halo was off. The weather channel was on. And every channel was running some story about the blizzard. There's been a giant snowball fight downtown—hundreds of participants over several hours. Power was out in large portions of Maryland. Targets were open; most other stores were not.

Most of all, though, were the updates that the cold spell was lingering, and so was the snow.

"Good thing we've got enough beer to last us through the week," I said. "See, Beth, I told you it was a good idea to buy that much."

Beth looked at Amber. "He seems to be under the impression that we can sustain ourselves on beer."

"And maybe chips and salsa," I added. "Sounds amazing."

"That's my husband: nutritional genius."

"Should I send you an invoice for my time?" I said.

It felt good getting these two beautiful women to laugh. Beth set her needles down, growing serious. "Hey, Jace, can I talk to you for a sec?"

"Sure." I waited, thinking that she meant here. Instead, she rose and started for the stairs.

"You coming?"

We went upstairs. I shut the door as Beth floated over to the windows, looking outside into the snowy landscape. The bright light from outside bathed her body like a glamor shot filter. For a second, I could imagine Beth posing for some soft-focus perfume ad, wearing the same skin-tight jeans and chic designer sweater she wore now. Her hair was loose, spilling in dark, textured waves around her shoulders. The light cast shadows across her high cheeks and full lips.

"Think we'll ever get out of here?" she asked, breaking the spell.

"Eventually. You know how the news is. *Snowpocolypse*? Really?

Don't worry, Beth. We've got enough food to feed the five of us."

Beth smiled, turning away from the window. Silhouetted like that—hair lit up like a halo—I couldn't see her face. "This isn't about that."

She was wringing her hands. Was she nervous?

When she stepped forward, I saw that look on her face; a smile tugged at the corners of her lips. Her eyes were wide and shimmering. No, not nervous. Excited.

"What is it, Beth?"

"I want to make everyone's fantasies come true."

"What?"

She floated over to me, setting her arms on my shoulders. Lifting onto her tip toes, she nuzzled my nose with hers. That serious look of excitement only grew more intense. "I've been thinking about it since this morning, actually. We're stuck in this house with people we love. I want to fulfill their fantasies."

"Amber's fling," I stated dumbly. I knew what she was saying, but I couldn't process it fast enough.

"Amber's fling with *you*. Yeah, that."

"You want me to...sleep with Amber?"

"You know I do. Especially if I can watch." She kissed me softly, just a brush of lips before pulling back. "I talked to her just now. She's game, too."

"Beth..."

"She and Paul talk about you all the time, apparently. You left an impression on that hot blonde—at least physically."

"And that doesn't make you jealous?"

Beth pressed herself against me. "Sort of. But mostly just really horny."

I laughed. "You've always been a giver."

"It's why you love me. You love how much I like to *give*." She teased her tongue along her lips, then burst out laughing.

"Okay. What about your fantasy?"

"Remember this morning, when you said that you were imagining me going down on him? When you came?"

Jealousy thundered through me. I felt it sizzle out to the tips of my hair before it passed, leaving in its wake a painfully hard cock.

"That's my fantasy, baby. Only instead of just me sucking his cock, I'm fucking him. And you're with me."

"This morning, when you came thinking of me with him, I was thinking the same thing." She brushed her hand across my jeans, squeezing the column of hard flesh.

"Fuck, Beth. You're killing me."

"I'm turning you on. It's a totally different thing."

"So what else? What else happens in your fantasy?"

I caught the beat of hesitation. I knew her well enough to know when she had something more to say. Thing about Beth is that she always shared, even when it was hard. "I want…" Was she actually blushing? "I want you both inside me. At the same time."

"Like…what?"

Beth took a deep breath. "I want to feel one of you in my pussy, and the other in my ass."

I forgot to breathe. I forgot how to speak. I just stared at her as I tried to figure out if what she'd just said was real or my twisted, fucked up imagination. Had my wife just told me she wanted to be DP'd? We'd tried anal a couple times, and I knew I hadn't been her first, but this was in an entirely different league.

For the longest time, we just stared at each other, wild-eyed and speechless.

"Say something, Jason. Are you upset?"

"No." The answer to that question was easy. "No way. God, it makes me so hot, just thinking about you…like that."

"Being taken by two strong men? Being crushed by all that hard testosterone? Being used like a fucking total slut?"

I wanted to say no to all of her questions—I wanted to deny the misogyny that they implied—but she'd been nothing but truthful, so I was, too. "I love you, Beth. I love how strong you are, and how smart. I'm in love with all of you, but yes. *Fucking hell,* yes. That would be so fucking hot."

Her lips crashed into mine, setting sweetness aside. Our tongues ravaged one another.

"Watching you and Paul snow-wrestle earlier today..." She kissed me again. "That sealed the deal. I wanted to be in the middle of that."

"You're not expecting..."

Beth giggled when she realized what I was implying. "No, I know you two don't swing that way." But then, she added a coy, "But it would be super hot if you did."

"*There's* a fantasy I'm not willing to fulfill this weekend."

"So you're game to do the others?"

I guess, although there was one that we hadn't talked about. Her being with Paul while I was there was one thing. Her being alone with Paul was different.

"What about Paul's?"

She nodded. "That too, but only if you're okay with it."

The jealousy was back, but I trusted her. And in some way, that taste of the forbidden was so damn arousing. "Yeah, I'm okay with it. After all, I'm going to be fucking his girlfriend... What about Casey? Don't you think she'll be a little left out?"

"Her fantasy was to watch us. I think she'll be fine."

"And what about mine? I never gave one."

Beth's smile oozed from cheek to cheek. "How about all of yours?"

"All of them? But you don't even know what they are."

"Baby, it doesn't matter. If I can help you fulfill it, and it's something you really want, then I'll do it. If not while we're snowed in, then later." She squeezed my cock. "Anything at all, you just tell me."

"Anything?"

"Want to watch me go down on Amber? She's never been with another woman, you know, but she's also curious. I could tell when we kissed."

"That would be hot."

"What about fucking her while *she* eats *me*? Or what about Casey?"

"She's like a sister—"

"None of that. No more denials. Do you want to fuck her? If that's your fantasy, I'll do my best to make that happen, too."

"Beth…"

"We better get back downstairs," she said with a cheeky smile.

"But…"

"Don't worry, honey. It's going to be amazing. Just follow my lead."

Chapter 7:
The Game Resumes

We managed to make it to four o'clock before we started drinking—a sure sign that we were no longer in college. We played through all our party games, but stopped once things got too competitive between Amber and Paul—he even accused Amber of cheating at Apples to Apples, something I'm pretty sure is impossible.

I kept wondering how Beth would shift things back to the sexual side of things.

Paul did it for her. "You know, Beth, Casey, and I never got to ask our questions last night."

"And I know exactly what I want to ask," Beth interjected, as if she'd made the point, not Paul. "Of the people in this room *that you haven't slept with already*, who are you most attracted to, and why?"

Very nicely done, Beth. That said, I didn't want to go first.

"I'll answer that one since I basically did yesterday," Paul said. "While I think you're a fucking babe, Case, we have too much history. So I'm definitely going with Beth here."

"But why?" Amber asked the question, hands on her hips and her mouth hard around the edges.

"Oh, come on, babe, don't be like that. You're hot and you know it. I guess that's part of it. I find her really attractive because she's so different from you. Beth's like—this is going to be a cliché, but fuck it. Beth's the girl-next-door. She's friendly, easy to talk to, and also—and this is the important piece—really good looking."

For an uncomfortable moment, I worried that Beth's plan had backfired. That Amber was going to storm off and throw Paul's things into the snow.

Instead, she smiled and sidled up to Beth. "Yeah, she *is* good looking, isn't she? Good kisser, too."

And just like that, like the two had planned it, they were kissing again. It lasted only about ten seconds, but it was long enough for them to share spit and get me hard.

Amber said, "Since I've slept with both of you boys, Beth's the one I'm most attracted to in this room. She's probably one of the coolest chicks I've ever met, not to mention her slammin' bod."

Beth hip checked her. "Please, stop teasing."

"Hey, Jason wasn't available, per your rules!"

I looked over at Casey, who was watching quietly from the edge of the room. That was more her MO: blending in, hiding behind her glasses, a fly on the wall. Since high school, she may have developed confidence beyond simply trendier glasses and more flattering clothes, but she was still the same girl I knew back then—the one who skipped junior prom because there was a rumor going around that the non-popular kids were going to vote her prom queen. I'd been on board; I always liked a good underdog story. But maybe I'd like this particular underdog, too.

"Feeling left out?" I asked her.

"Not at all. Does that sound like me?" Casey said. She adjusted her glasses and smiled.

"No. You like to hide."

"Now you're sounding like my boyfriend," she said.

"So he *is* your boyfriend!" That almost changed what I was about to say. Almost. "Well, hope he doesn't mind, but you're my pick."

"Oh, how flattering. Between me and Paul, I'm honored."

That's right, Amber and Beth were not options. "You're a pretty good consolation prize."

She mock-curtsied. "Why thank you."

"Your turn."

"Hmm. So many choices." She tapped a finger on her lips and looked around the room. "Who am I most attracted to..."

I felt hot as she lingered on me. Truth was, I would have picked her over Amber.

She addressed her question to Paul and I. "I suppose what you'd like to hear is that I've always wanted some fantasy threesome between you guys, huh? Well, I'm sorry to say that it was totally platonic back then."

Was that a pause before she said *back then*?

She looked at Beth and Amber. "The first time I met you was at Beth's wedding—my first wedding as an adult. And God, you were so beautiful. You were actually the first woman I'd ever fantasized about...I mean *really* fantasized about."

"Really?" Beth said.

"I'd always been curious, and I'd had plenty of opportunities while in college and traveling around, and all that. But I never really thought about it seriously until I saw you glowing in that white dress."

"Wow. I don't know what to say."

"But you aren't who I'm most attracted to."

Casey set her sights on Amber, who gasped and blushed bright. "I mean, come on, how can I not go for the tall, leggy blonde? You're so beautiful, and Beth did a pretty good job picking out her bridesmaid dresses."

"I actually helped pick them out," Amber said, fighting down a blush.

Casey smiled. "Then thank you. And I think some random dude at the wedding has a lot to thank you for, too."

Amber didn't seem to know where to look. She glanced at Paul a lot, at me, but every time she looked at Casey, she blushed and looked away. Finally, she said, "So Beth, you going to answer?"

I turned to my wife, curious about her answer myself.

"I'm not going to prioritize my friends. Truth is, I'm attracted to all of you." She lingered on all three of them before giggling. "And I've definitely fantasized about all three of you, too." To Amber, she nodded. "Yes, even you, my bestie."

If this group wasn't sexually charged now, we never would be.

"I'm going to heat up some left overs," Beth said to the silent room. Amber offered to help, leaving the original three alone.

Casey spoke first. "So I take it you two are over your little thing?"

After Beth's round of questioning, I couldn't even remember what I was so mad about.

"Jason's the one who attacked me," Paul said defensively.

Oh, that's right.

"I seem to recall something about a snow boulder hitting me in the face, bud," I said. "You've got nothing to do with that?"

Casey chuckled. "Guess there's still a thing."

Her phone rang before she could say more. "It's The Boyfriend. You two get some beers and get this out of your system. You're going to fuck up the whole night if you don't."

She headed for the stairs, putting an exaggerated swing in her hips. She looked great in those skinny jeans. Into the phone, she laughed. Said: "No, this is the *perfect* time to call."

When she was gone, Paul said, "Yeah, Casey's all grown up, isn't she? How could we have missed that body?"

"Because she's like a sister to us?" I said weakly. I wasn't thinking about her like a sister at that moment.

"So...beers?"

We didn't bother putting on jackets when we went outside to the keg. I pumped from the door as Paul held the nozzle to our cups, filling them with a golden, frothy microbrew.

"So Amber's pretty pissed at you," I said. Easiest way to mend guy-fences? Talk about chick problems.

"Would you believe it if I told you she isn't as confident as she comes across?"

"Yeah, I'd believe it." Hell, I knew it.

"I'm sorry I said that last night. About Beth."

An apologizing Paul was a rare thing. But I also knew not to make a big deal about it, so I waved it off. "We were drunk. Things were said."

"Yeah..." He nodded, lost in thought. At last, he said the thing that must have been on his mind all day: "That story that Amber told..."

Here we go. Awkward conversation incoming.

"It's a little fucked up, isn't it?" He didn't look back, just kept on filling our cups. I let him talk. "I just sat there as she flirted with this random guy, right? And..." He forced a laugh. "And it made me hard. I thought: *so this is what she was like back in college?* And it was really hot, watching her in action like that."

With both our cups filled, he finally had to turn around. "You must think I'm some kind of wimp, but fuck it. I didn't feel like one when I watched."

Paul and I had been friends since grade school, but we never opened up like this. He needed a bone to be thrown, so I tried my best.

"Pretty sure you're not the only guy who's had that fantasy."

"Have you?"

"With Beth? Sure. This weekend more than ever. Hearing about some of the things in the past—"

"Has you thinking about the present?" Paul finished.

"Something like that. Beth's an incredible woman. I've always had fun with her, but it's always been in the context of the two of us. Hearing about some of her other adventures has shown me a new side of her. And I kind of want to see that."

"I hear ya. It's the same with me. Kind of. You ever think she'd...I don't know...relive some of those old adventures?"

"Not really. Not without me, anyway. I trust her more than I trust myself, you know?"

"You should. I've tried, believe me."

"Go fuck yourself." We went back into the living room where I worked on the fire a little. I knew the next question I wanted to ask, but it took a few swallows of beer before I could. "So did you want it to go further?"

"Amber seemed to." He didn't answer the question, and for a second, I didn't think he would. He surprised me. "I don't know. I think, maybe? Fucked up, huh?"

"So out there, when you asked me about Beth reliving past adventures, you were really wondering about Amber."

"Yeah. And the craziest thing? I kind of don't want to be part of it. It'd be, I don't know, hotter if she just did it."

"Without permission."

"Yeah. I guess. Fuck, I don't know."

I glanced at my friend. He was sitting on the couch, staring into space. Thinking about what could have been? I wasn't sure how to respond to this incarnation of Paul. I wasn't sure that he was even expecting a response.

Amber and Beth returned with plates of microwaved leftovers and a couple bottles of wine. I followed Beth back to the kitchen to help her bus out the rest.

"This feels like a vacation," Beth beamed, snatching a cube of cheese off the wooden platter I had.

I kissed her cheese tasting lips through that silly smile. "A fantasy vacation for Paul, apparently...stuck with his dream girl and all."

"Paul likes me? I hadn't noticed." She batted her lashes. "How're you doing, Jace? That doesn't really make you upset, does it?"

"Nah. I think I've figured it out, mostly. Paul and I have been friends forever, and I love him to death, but he can be a really self-centered ass sometimes. Ever since we were in first grade, he's been wanting my stuff—anything that I had and he didn't, he wanted."

"Oh, so I'm now *stuff*?"

I squeezed her ass, feeling the scant lines of a thong through the stretchy black material. "*My* stuff, specifically."

"And you can think of no other reason why he'd want me."

"I can think of plenty of reasons. But the Stuff Thing is probably the main one."

Beth rolled her eyes with a smile. "You really know how to make a girl feel special."

I kissed her forehead. "That's why they call me a romantic."

"Come on, Prince Charming, let's get back in there."

****

Like last night, we ate dinner around the coffee table in front of the fireplace, its flames snapping in the background.

Casey joined us just as we started to settle. She'd changed into the pajamas that she'd brought—a comfortable pair of flannel pants, a tank top, and her grey hoodie. She still carried her phone in her hand, along with a secretive smile.

"Your boyfriend?" Paul asked.

"Yeah. He says hi. And he wishes he was here." Again, that smile. "So we ready to get back to our questions? It's just me and Paul left. Paul, I have the feeling that you've been dying to ask yours all day. Go for it."

Paul grinned. "You know me so well, Case. Okay, friends and lovers, I want to know everyone's craziest sexual experiences."

Chapter 8:
Craziest Sexual Experiences

Craziest sexual experiences. Of course he wanted those. That was Paul, pretty generic as these games go. That wasn't to say I was unhappy with the question. Between Casey's surprisingly healthy sex life and everything that I was learning about my own wife, it could have possibly been the perfect question.

I glanced at Beth, wondering what tale she'd tell, and whether it would feature me or someone else. After last night, I was kind of hoping for the latter.

"I'll go first," I said, breaking the ice—although after all that was going on, coupled with the beer and wine, there was very little ice to break. "Amber's already heard this one, I think, but you three haven't."

"Ooh...does it involve you two?" Beth asked, looking from the blonde to me. Honestly, did the woman get jealous at all?

"No, but it was in college. In our sophomore year."

Amber's face split into a smile as she figured it out.

"We'd already had our thing and, thankfully, were still friends. So Amber introduced me to this exchange student from England.

God, I loved that accent..."

"And she was a redhead, too," Amber pointed out.

"Yeah..."

I had this very vivid image of her in my mind: her soft, coppery ringlets falling around her round face—flushed from our latest bout of lovemaking. I remembered the way that hair covered her pale breasts like a figure from a Romantic era painting, and I remember how a strand of it had caught in her full, glossy lips.

Beth, who was sitting next to me, drove her elbow into my side—a friendly reminder that she was there and I had a story to tell.

"Sorry, erm...where was I?"

"Redhead. British. College?" Beth helped me out.

"Right. So a bunch of us decided to go out to Virginia Beach on a lark and do the bonfire thing. I think there was some drinking that preceded this decision. We carpooled: two cars and Amber's boyfriend's pickup. Long story short, there was more drinking, some weed, some skinny dipping if I recall...'

Amber nodded.

"And, as these things go, organization broke down."

The drive from school to beach was longer than we'd thought, and being stupid kids, we hadn't thought it all the way through. I had a great time, but not everyone did—namely, the designated drivers. When the drivers of the two cars announced that they were going home, four of us decided to stay—me and my latest girl, Amber and her boyfriend. It hadn't really occurred to me that logistically, this wasn't going to work out so well in our favor.

"When the four of us were finally ready to go home, we realized the mistake," I continued. "So this British chick grabs the blankets we'd been sitting on, hopped into the bed of the pick-up, and patted the spot next to her. Amber and her boy-toy got in the cab, and off we went!"

"So far, I'm not getting the *craziest* part of the whole question."

"It's coming," Amber answered for me.

"Yeah," I grinned. "It was late. Maybe 1:30 in the morning, and the drive was going to be a long one. This girl and I had been flirting and playing with each other all night—not to mention that I'd skinny dipped with a bunch of sexy coeds. So I was horny, and I wasn't alone."

It hadn't been my idea, and I remember being nervous when she'd whispered it to me, but I didn't share that part of the tale with my friends. She'd put my mind at ease by shifting down under the blankets, fishing my cock out, and taking it into her mouth.

"Before I know what's going on, we're both naked in the bed of this pick-up, racing down the highway at seventy miles an hour and fucking each other silly." I had to laugh at the surprised look on Beth's face.

"Wow. Did you know?" she asked Amber.

"Only later, although I think I said something about the truck's suspension needing to be checked?"

We all laughed.

"Anyone want to hit the beach now?" Paul added.

Beth answered. "While I don't mind a bikini in this weather, a hot tub is a requirement."

Casey and Amber began to clear the dishes and refill our drinks.

"That's some story," Paul said.

"It was definitely fun."

"Puts a whole new meaning to a quickie," he said.

"Oh, there was nothing quick about it."

Beth snuggled up to me. "Can our next car be a pick-up?"

"Wouldn't you rather Paul get the pick-up?" I asked.

Beth looked across at our friend. "Paul, you want to pick me up?"

"You know it." His grin was less predatory than it had been last night.

"I'm going to change into my pajamas, if that's cool," I said. "Casey's got me jealous."

Beth rose with me. "Isn't Casey supposed to be getting *me* jealous?"

I held my response until we were alone upstairs. I closed the door and turned to my wife. "You're not actually jealous of Casey, are you?"

"Do I get jealous?" She pulled her shirt off, quickly distracting me with her bra-encased tits.

"I didn't think so. Do you?"

The bra went next, but she coyly turned her back to me, hiding her charms. "Should I be? You're not about to confess that you and Casey have—"

"No! She's like my sister." I'd been saying that long enough that I almost believed it.

Beth wasn't so easily fooled.

"I didn't know you lusted after your sisters. Naughty boy."

Down went her pants, leaving her in nothing but that thong I'd felt earlier.

"That's too bad. I bet she's fun." The smile she tossed my direction over her shoulder was priceless. "Too bad about her boyfriend, too. It's been years since I've been with another woman."

I walked up behind Beth, wrapping my arms around her nearly naked body. She was on fire. "Is that something you think about a lot? Other women?"

"I thought we covered this last night."

I pressed. "But you do. It makes you wet, doesn't it?" I slipped my hand into her panties. She was practically dripping.

"Ah, Jace…" Beth stiffened as I ran my middle finger along her slit. I could have fucked her right then and there, she was so wet.

"Tell me. Do you ever think about other women when you play with yourself?"

She groaned, driving her butt into my hard-on. "Think I pretty much admitted that down there, didn't I?"

"So you and Casey?" I added a second finger to her cunt.

She peeled the thong down her thighs, freeing my hand to work. "Tell me you haven't, and so will I."

"You little nympho."

"Ha…*oh*." Her laugh broke into a moan. I played my thumb across her clit. She shuddered. "What can I say? I'm a sucker for dark hair and light eyes."

"And big tits?"

Beth leaned her head onto my shoulder. "I think that's more of a guy thing, but sure, I noticed those, too."

"And *Amber*? Your best friend?"

"From the second I saw her. Casey's right, she's one of the most beautiful women I've ever met. I mean, you *know*. You've fucked her."

She wiggled out of my arms and went for her dresser. I expected her to pull out her standard issue pajamas—comfortable and practical—and while she did grab those, she also slid into a pink satin thong that I associated more with date night than comfort.

"What?" she asked when she saw me looking.

"Never seen you wear a thong to bed. At least not when you weren't looking for sex."

She yanked out her pink-and-white striped pajama bottoms—synonymous with Victoria's Secret—and looked at me over her bare shoulder. "So maybe I'm looking for sex."

She pulled out her matching bra—pink satin edged in white lace filigree—then went for the button-up top. She turned with it still open. "Honey, if you're even a little bit hesitant about...the whole fantasy thing, then it's off, okay?"

I glanced into her open shirt, loving the way that bra presented her cute breasts. I wouldn't be the only one admiring that view. The realization sank in with equal parts terror and excitement.

Beth read me again. "Let's come up with a code word. If either of us gets uncomfortable with anything, say..."

"*Marzipan.*"

Beth laughed. "How about something less weird, although I appreciate the creativity. How about *apples and oranges*?"

"Boring."

She touched my face, a faux frown on hers. "Really? You think I'm boring?"

"Good point."

Kissing me, she buttoned up her shirt and patted my chest. "See you down there. *Apples and oranges.* Remember it."

"I will, but I don't think I'll need it."

If Beth heard my lack of total confidence, she didn't indicate it beyond a quick look. And then she was gone.

Alone, getting dressed in my flannel pants and faded t-shirt, I said aloud, "Apples and oranges, what the hell am I doing?"

Chapter 9:
Casey's Fantasy

I spent the longest time up there in our room, alone. Or it felt like long, anyway. Truth was, I *was* hesitant about the fantasy fulfillment thing—at least a little. I loved the idea of Beth's wild past, and at least a part of me was into the idea of bringing that past into the present.

I wasn't like Paul. I didn't want her fucking around without me knowing about it. For Paul, there was a sense of masochism to his fantasy—he wanted to be wronged. For me, I liked that other people thought Beth was hot—and I loved discovering her crazier side.

Yet the thought of that had my stomach churning. So maybe I was more like Paul than I thought.

When I finally emerged from the bedroom, I wasn't any more clear on what I wanted to happen, but at least I had a code word in my back pocket and a newfound sense of sexual adventure.

Amber and Paul had also changed into their pajamas, although since they hadn't come prepared to spend the night at all, Paul's sleepwear consisted of an old pair of my pants that didn't quite cover his ankles and his t-shirt from yesterday.

Amber fared better, being the same size as my wife—although

Amber would have looked good in a floor-length night gown. She'd put on one of Beth's sleep shirts, coupling them with a pair of my wife's gray knit knee-high socks. Up until that moment, I'd never considered them sexy. On the blonde's legs, everything changed.

"Okay, so who's next?" Paul asked. "Tell me your craziest sexual experience."

Beth and Casey left a spot on the sectional and I happily took my position between the two pretty brunettes. When I was comfortably seated, Beth leaned across me and said to Casey, "Jason would like to hear about your threesome."

"Thanks a lot," I said to my wife as Casey grinned at me.

Beth patted my knee. "No problem, dear."

Casey scooted into the corner of the couch, turning to regard me without being super close. "Well, you're in luck, Jace, because even considering what went down in Vegas, that threesome was probably the craziest thing I've ever done."

Paul clapped his hands together. "Let's hear it."

Casey took a swallow of her wine. She still wore her hoodie, but had it unzipped and open around her generous cleavage. I couldn't help myself from looking, and when I did, I saw that her hard nipples making points in her tight top.

"Okay, let's see... It was my junior year at MIT. I'd been seeing these two guys for a few weeks—one went to BU, can't remember where the other went. Neither of them were the sharpest crayons in the box, but they made up for it in bed."

Her smile was like a puddle of spilled molasses, spreading slowly wider.

"Anyway, they didn't know about each other—not that I kept it a secret or anything, just...neglected to tell, you know? Then, Valentine's Day came around. It almost turned out to be a disaster. Both guys decided to surprise me, showing up at my apartment with a dozen roses and the same damn box of chocolates! If they'd have come, you know, even a half hour apart, I would've been fine. But they showed up within minutes of each other."

"Well that's a nightmare," Beth said.

"Tell me about it. Those two guys were like, *What the hell?* Before they could really put it all together—like I said, we're not talking geniuses here—I dragged them into the apartment, cracked open a bottle of wine that I'd been planning on enjoying alone, and made some of the most awkward introductions of my life. I mean, what could I say? *Tom, meet Eric, he likes me doggy-style. Eric, meet Tom, who prefers coming on my face.*"

Beth cracked up. "Wow. So what happened?"

"As it turns out, they *did* kind of start comparing notes. I think they were remarking on how slutty I was, I don't know. Something about being always ready and willing. One of them suggested that I was probably willing right then. And that's how it all kind of started."

Casey pulled her hoodie off. "Getting hot in here. Anyone else feel that?" Her golden skin glowed in the flickering firelight, soft and smooth.

"And it was good?" Beth asked. She snuggled closer to me and I wrapped my arm around her. I could practically feel her heart racing. Or was that mine?

On the sofa, Paul and Amber had cuddled up, too, and were now sharing the blanket.

"Like I said, it was intense to be taken like that—and I was definitely taken. So much testosterone! I'm a rough sex kind of girl, and Tom and Eric were both used to that." Her tight cotton top pulled close around her full breasts, where her nipples cast small shadows. "I just wasn't prepared for twice the helping, you know?"

"Did they take turns?" Beth whispered. "Or...?" She looked over at me quickly, but I pretended not to notice.

When Casey leaned forward to grab a wedge of cheese off the coffee table, I couldn't help looking into her generous cleavage. I don't think anyone could.

"Oh yeah." She popped the cheese into her mouth. "It was definitely a threesome, not back-to-back twosomes."

"God..."

I pushed my hand beneath Beth's top, rolling the warm metal of her navel piercing between my fingers. On the sofa, Paul's hands we're definitely roaming beneath the blanket.

"How crazy did things get?" Paul asked.

Casey laughed. "Well, Tom definitely got his doggy-style while Eric came on my face. And then we switched. The guys wanted to try DPing me, but that seemed a little crazy, even for me."

I fought the urge to look at Beth.

"DPing?" Amber asked.

"Double penetration. You know, one in my ass, one in my pussy."

"Sounds scary," Amber said.

"Yeah. Anal's something where I need a guy's complete trust. They were throwing me around like two dogs with a rawhide bone. I wasn't about to let them go there."

Beth's breath caught as I dipped my hand lower, pulling open the drawstring of her pants. She caught my hand and gave a quick head shake. I relented, coming to my senses.

"Still have that fantasy?" I whispered into her ear.

"Hell. Yeah."

The wet, muted smacks drew our attention to the couch, where Amber and Paul were making out. Amber's hand moved vigorously beneath the blanket, just over Paul's lap.

"God, I wish I had someone here," Casey said beside me. I thought about reaching out and pulling her close. The fire popped. I didn't move.

"Want to know what my wildest experience was?" Beth asked Casey directly.

"Please."

Beth climbed into my lap, shifting until her pussy rubbed against my clothed cock. Casey didn't miss the positioning, but didn't say anything, either.

Facing out, Beth twisted, putting her hand around my neck. She looked across at Amber and Paul, who were still kissing, seemingly oblivious to what my wife was saying. Beth said, "I'm going to guess this is also going to be Amber's craziest experience, too."

Apparently, Amber *was* listening. She broke off her kiss. Her lips were pink, her hair mussed. "If this is the story I think it is, then yes. It's never gotten wilder than that."

Beth nodded. "So at the sorority house, we weren't allowed to have boys in our rooms. Weird rule, but all the sisters followed it." She slowly undulated in my lap, stimulating my cock. "That's why we never had many guys over."

Thinking back on it, I realized that I never saw the inside of Beth's room—or Amber's.

Beth continued. "If we did want to hook up, though, we had a room in the basement..." Amber's moan drifted lazily across the room. I didn't look, even though I wanted to. I got all the information I needed from the look on Casey's face when *she* did.

Beth continued. "There were some couches down there. A TV. No windows. There are some crazy stories about that room, but I've only ever used it once."

I trembled.

In my lap, she squirmed. "I was with this guy I'd been seeing for a while. We'd just come back from dinner when it started pouring outside."

"Were you two intimate?" The words spilled out.

Beth smirked at my old-fashioned way of asking. "Yes, Shawn and I had had sex before." She glanced back at me, applying more pressure against my erection. "A lot of sex."

My chest tightened along with my balls.

"That particular night, we were horny and looking for a place to hook up. The house was pretty empty, most girls out at parties. I took him into the basement."

The air grew thicker. I ran my hands around her hips and up her back. Up under her top. Her soft skin was clammy and her breathing came short in my ear. "It was dark when we walked in. We didn't realize it wasn't empty..."

"Haaahh..." Amber's moan drifted across the room, surfing on the heavy air.

"We heard them first. The sound was unmistakable. A squishy, wet slapping, you know?"

"Uh!" The blonde's sharp cry drew my attention off my wife's low voice. I had to look.

Amber sat straddling Paul's lap, her legs draped on either side. The blanket covered the lower halves and her night shirt was still in place, but there was no doubt what they were doing. Not with the way Amber rolled her hips, or the look of pained concentration on Paul's face.

Jesus. They were fucking?

Beth reached behind her and freed her hair from its ponytail. It cascaded around her, splashing around her face and off her shoulders. My lungs filled with her heady scent. She continued, her voice as thick as the air around us. "When our eyes adjusted, we saw them. Amber and her boyfriend."

The room had filled with a hazy, orange glow as the fire died out. Shadows danced on the other couple as their bodies rippled and steamed.

Amber shifted, grasping the hem of her night shirt. It was a snug fit, but she managed to peel it off with grace. I should have looked away.

Should have, but could not. Would not.

I fed on the sight of her large, perfectly formed breasts. Paul cradled one gently as though offering it to me. Her puckered, pale nipples screamed.

Beth continued to gyrate in my lap. She twisted around and kissed me, slow and hot. When she continued, she seemed to be talking to me alone.

"Not a word was spoken. We watched for a little while from the other couch, but then it was too much. He was hard. I was horny..."

"Yeah?"

"Want to know what happened next?"

I nodded. Casey's practically moaned her *yes.*

"Let me show you."

Kissing me one last time, she slipped off my lap and settled between my legs. Her irises caught in the firelight, bronze stars that twinkled as she looked over the contours of my cock. She chewed her lip as she eased me out of my flannel pants.

Even in my expanding lungs, the air felt heavy. The more I breathed, the shorter of breath I got. Was this happening? Was this really fucking happening?

"Nghhh!" Just a few feet away, Amber stiffened in Paul's lap, her back arching, her eyes tightly closed. The blanket slipped until it just barely covered her pelvis. She had a tattoo low on her right hip— a songbird with musical notes floating from its beak. Very twisted Disney.

My cock hit the balmy, open air for a second before Beth rolled her warm tongue up one side and down the other. I gasped.

Paul's eyes found us on the opposite couch, although our gazes never touched. Was he watching Beth's ass, squatting on the floor? Or her bouncing head as she took me into her mouth? It was my engorged thickness that was passing into Beth's throat, so why was it me who suddenly felt choked?

She teased me with slow, measured strokes, holding me firmly at the base as she faded off. Her lips formed a gliding, velvet ring. Up and down. Root to head to root.

She pulled off. I sighed.

"Are you okay with this?" she asked.

I nodded, but when I opened my eyes, I realized that the question wasn't for me.

"It's a little late to be asking that," Casey said. "But I'm definitely okay."

As if to prove it, Casey pulled her cami top off, freeing her generous tits. They were probably the same size as Amber's—a healthy C cup, bordering on more—but on her smaller body, they looked huge.

Our eyes met. Casey winked at me. I felt the weight of the moment as we crashed through the barrier of Just Friends.

Amber's loud climax shattered the connection. Our heads snapped to the blonde just as she stiffened in orgasm. The blanket had slipped to the floor, leaving nothing concealed. Their hips rode the edge of the couch, bodies reclined. Entangled.

Paul's cock looked huge, bowing up and into Amber's hairless pussy. It was almost obscene, how stretched and full she looked around him. I wanted to look away but could not. I was hypnotized by the way those bare petals pulled as she ascended, unwilling to let him go, and how she swallowed him up with each rapid descent.

I wondered what all that nonsense about me being bigger was. That dispelled my theory that Paul's machismo was a product of a small-dick complex.

Paul fucked her hard through her rising orgasm, yanking her

against him by her tits. She twisted back, their mouths finding one another in a sloppy kiss. She gasped, unable to maintain it, and moaned through the last of her release.

Beth, who'd been slowly tugging on my cock, took her hand away long enough to unbutton her shirt. "God, that's hotter than I remembered."

With her shirt hanging open, her perky tits presented over the top of her bra, her mouth descended on my cock again. She held me steady with both hands and attacked.

"Watch them, baby," Beth whispered, her tongue carving a meandering zigzag along the outside of my cock. "Amber's definitely multi-orgasmic. At least she was that night."

The head of my saliva-bathed member carved a bulge into her cheek as she took me back into her mouth. I did as I was told.

"Oh, I'm still definitely multi-orgasmic," Amber said. Her husky voice tantalized. "You remember, don't you, Jason?"

The couple had shifted back on the sofa with Amber leaning forward, relieving some of the pressure. She braced herself on Paul's splayed knees, slowly working her hips into his lap like a stripper. She gasped as Paul sent a sharp thrust through her. I could see his face tighten behind her, his teeth clenching.

"That is so hot." Casey's voice was tight. I followed her voice to my right, finding that the brunette had shed her pajama pants as well. She had her hand down the front of her thong, the flimsy material doing nothing to hide what she was doing. "So what happened next?"

Amber picked up on the story. "I don't think that I even noticed that I had an audience until I came. Then I noticed Beth and Shawn—and Beth just going nuts on him..."

Beth renewed her energy on my cock, sucking harder, bobbing faster. Shawn's name sent a spike of something cold yet exciting through me. Once insinuated, I couldn't shake the image of her doing this to another man—and I didn't even know what Shawn looked like.

"I'm not sure what was hotter, having an audience, or watching Beth blow him like a fucking porn star."

"Oh, God..." I groaned, feeling my orgasm bear down on me.

Amber continued, seeming to know just how to push my buttons. "I'd heard that she was pretty good at giving head. She'd developed a rep with some of the guys we knew."

I looked down at Beth, who was watching me carefully as she put on a demonstration of just how good she was.

"It was inspiring to watch her. She really...loves doing that."

I looked back at Amber and Paul. They'd begun to fuck again. She leaned forward, arms braced on the coffee table as Paul took her in an awkward doggy-style.

"Beth loves giving head so much that..." She paused, moaning gently. "That when I offered my boyfriend's cock to her, she didn't even hesitate."

I came, so fast and abrupt that even Beth wasn't prepared to take the blast. She choked, taking a stream of come across her cheek before she was able to regain control. Covering my cock, she swallowed the rest of what I had. Swallowing like she had Shawn. Like she had Beth's boyfriend—a total stranger.

"Yeah, Paul. You like that story, too?" Amber said. The empty glasses littering the table's surface rattled with each thrust. "I bet you do. I bet you like hearing about how another man fucked me."

As the action shifted back to our friends, Beth wiped her face, emptied the contents of her wine, and sloshed it inside her mouth before swallowing. She crawled into my lap and rested her forehead right up against mine.

Are we okay? she seemed to ask.

I nodded, although my brain was alive with questions and uncertainties. So Beth had this crazy past—crazier than I'd imagined. So what? She was still the same woman I'd fallen in love with—that I'd married. If I could just stop and process it for one minute, I'd realize that none of it was all that surprising.

But I didn't have a minute. And nothing about this night could be stopped.

"Look," Beth whispered, glancing not at Amber and Paul, but at Casey.

Right beside us, Casey was going for it. She was tweaking one of her tits in her hand while the other was moving furiously inside her thong. Her body, naked and glowing with a satin sheen of sweat, was sexier than anything I'd ever imagined. I'd seen her in a bathing suit, but that was back in high school. The Casey of today was a bombshell: full tits with tiny, dark nipples, a narrow waist and flat belly, pierced with a dangling piece of silver jewelry, hips that flared enough to give her an ass and curves that could be called hourglass.

"God, she's hot," Beth whispered. "She's definitely stirring up some buried desires." Beth's hand fell on my cock as she said it, just in time to feel it begin to come back to life.

Beth stood, stripping off her unbuttoned top. Her bottoms were gone and with a quick shimmy of her shoulders, she stood before us in her pink satin lingerie.

"You know, we haven't even told you the craziest part of that night," Beth said. "Want to hear?"

I did, but I didn't. I knew what was coming next. I could put it all together. It was sweet torture. "Please."

"After I blew Shawn, I needed to do something to get him hard again. I so needed to get fucked." She looked at Casey, not me, her eyes flicking down between the brunette's legs, where her fingers were pumping herself. "I knew exactly how to get him going—how to get all men going again, right...Casey?"

The other brunette nodded with a smile. And then I watched Beth lower herself over Casey, bracing one hand on the back of the sofa and the other on Casey's face. Beth leaned in and their lips met in a sweet, gentle kiss. I went from semi-erect to mostly-ready in the span of that kiss. Christ, really?

As if hearing my question, the women returned for a second kiss, this one quickly melting into something longer and deeper. They tipped their heads in that practiced way that experienced kissers do, opening their mouths and letting their tongues roam.

Beth broke it off, looking over at me—at my erect cock. To Casey, she whispered, "Thank you."

Casey adjusted her glasses, which had gone a bit askew with the kiss. "I can think of a few ways for you to thank me."

"Is that an invitation?" Beth asked lightly.

"Please."

I could barely keep up with what was happening. Beth kissed Casey once again—a slower, longer kiss—as her hand slipped from the other woman's face down her neck Beth cupped Casey's tit, her thumb tweaking her nipple. Casey moaned against Beth, their kiss continuing.

Across the way, Amber and Paul had slowed their pace. She was still bent over the coffee table, her tits swinging beneath her, but Paul wasn't pounding her. They were as mesmerized in the spectacle beside me as I was.

Beth kissed down Casey's body, sliding down until she could take one of the other woman's nipples into her mouth.

Amber said, "We didn't go that far." She almost sounded wistful.

Beth pulled off Casey, looking back at her friend. "One of my biggest regrets."

She didn't wait for a response. She went right back to Casey, slipping to the floor and opening the other woman's thighs. Looking up at Casey, Beth said, "Watch them. Enjoy it."

With that, Beth pulled Casey's thong to the side. I caught a flash of glistening pink before Beth lowered her mouth.

I wrapped my hand around my cock, pumping it slowly as I watched Beth go down on another woman. My head spun. My mind reeled. Yet when Beth looked up at Casey, tugged at her thong, and said, "Let's take this off," it was my wife's familiar voice making the suggestion.

"Shaved," Beth said, running her thumb across Casey's bald mound. "Naughty, naughty."

"Waxed, actually. Just a couple days ago."

"Mmm, even better." Beth lifted Casey's legs over her shoulders. Pressing her middle and index fingers together, she twisted them around and deftly pushed them into Casey's pussy. Her tongue fell on the other woman's clit a beat later. The timing was so perfect, so fluid, that any doubt that this was her first time was gone.

Casey raked her fingers through Beth's hair, moaning as my wife went to work on her. "Uh, God, oh my...God!"

Beth lifted her mouth from Casey's sex long enough to ask, "Are you watching Amber and Paul? Because as good as your pussy tastes, I wouldn't want to deprive you of your all-time fantasy of watching another couple."

Casey giggled. "I can multi-task, don't worry." To Amber and Paul, who'd slowed their pace, she said, "Give me a show."

Paul didn't need any further encouragement. He rose up onto his haunches, bending Amber deeper over the coffee table as he took her. She braced herself on her elbows, her beautiful face grimacing with each heavy thrust.

Paul fucked like an animal. He slapped her ass. He pulled her hair. He used her body more than made love to it. He used it while all the while staring at my wife—stripped down to her pink bra and thong—as she ate out another woman.

I couldn't get comfortable. Not with the way that he eye-fucked my wife. Not with the way he took Amber. Certainly not with that tickle of an idea that he'd be fucking Beth this way at some point before we got out of this house. And yet I was harder than I'd ever been all night—something that had almost no connection to Beth's tongue in Casey's pussy.

As I watched Paul drill Amber, I forced the issue. Could I take him doing this to Beth? Did I secretly want that?

Fucking hell, yes, I did.

I dialed back my stroking as the two sets of lovers neared release. Casey tried to watch Paul and Amber, but her eyes glazed over as Beth worked her magic. She gritted her teeth and reclined against the sofa. Beth's tongue danced across her pussy; her fingers curled inward and upward, hitting Casey's g-spot over and over until she shattered her world.

"Ah—AH!" Casey screamed as she came, her legs twisting around Beth's head, ankles locked. Beth had to yank free or suffocate, her thumb replacing her mouth as she milked the tail end of Casey's orgasm.

When Beth looked up at me, she looked sheepish. *So that happened*, she seemed to say. I wanted to grab her and take her hard at that embarrassed smile alone, but before I could do anything, Amber's cry reminded us that we weren't alone.

"Is that all you've got?" Amber's challenge sliced through the rising aria of moans and gasps. "Do I need to find a real man to fuck me?"

Paul redoubled his efforts, his fingers squeezing her hips so tightly that he left white marks in her skin.

"Jason over there looks ready to take care of me. Aren't you, Jace?"

I looked at Beth, who gave a short nod. God, I loved this woman.

"Always," I said.

Amber twisted out of Paul's grasp, turning swiftly to shove him back into the love seat. She crawled over him, long limbs over his muscled body. With her face in his, his cock in her hand, she stared him down.

"This is mine. You don't get to touch it unless I say so. Got it?"

"You can't tell me—"

"Fuck that, Paul. I'm tired of your contradictions. You can't tell me you want something, then deny me. You can't get all fucking turned on watching me flirt with other men, only to yank me back. It turns *me* on, too. There have been other Andrews, you know. There are always Andrews—guys out there wanting nothing more than a quick, no-strings-attached fuck. And you know what? The next time one of them asks and I'm interested, I'm going to do it."

She looked over her shoulder at me. I knew my role.

"I'm feeling a little left out," I said. "Want to help me out?"

She smiled, kissed Paul one last time, and rose out of his lap. "I was hoping you'd ask…"

Amber was the epitome of hot: long, wavy blonde hair, pale skin, full breasts and hips wide enough to suggest the proverbial hourglass. I thought she was beautiful back in college, but the last five years had transformed her into the woman that she was.

And that woman was about to fuck me.

She sauntered around the coffee table, her hips swaying with purpose. I thought those knee-high knit socks looked good before, but in the firelight on Amber's otherwise naked body, they were as sexy as stockings.

"He's staring at me, Paul," Amber said without taking her eyes off me. "He's making me so wet."

Behind her, Paul's hand twitched for his cock, but he kept them by his side.

"I'm going to suck his cock. You like that idea, Paul? You ready to watch me give another man a blowjob?"

His *yes* caught in his throat.

Beside me, Beth had crawled up beside Casey. The two women snuggled, cheek to cheek—it was almost innocent, had Beth not been absently stroking one of Casey's nipples.

Amber sank to her knees. "Long time, Jace," Amber said. And without further adieu, she dropped her mouth over my length and took me down to the hilt. I passed fluidly into her throat—something I don't remember her being able to do that last time we were together. Glancing at Paul and his towering erection, it wasn't hard to figure out where she'd picked up the new skill.

The smacking of lips drew my attention to the women beside me, who were making out again. Beth's hand had drifted down between Casey's legs, and as I looked on, Casey's did the same—sliding beneath Beth's thong.

Between that girl-on-girl show and Amber's skilled blowjob, I nearly lost it. Shuddering, I squeezed my eyes shut and forced my thoughts away from anything sexual. Shoveling the snow. Doing laundry. What were we going to do when we ran out of beer...?

None of it helped. All it took was an "Uh, God!" from Beth, and I was right back in the present, sitting next to her as she was fingered by another woman.

Amber pulled away, driving her thumb into my perineum to shut off my release before it started. I groaned. I bucked. But somehow, miraculously, I didn't come.

"No need to waste that," Amber said, rising over me. "I want to feel you come inside of me, not in my mouth."

She rose, swinging her leg over mine. To Paul, she asked, "I bet you're ready to play with yourself now, aren't you?"

She was baiting him, and he didn't grace her with a response. Even in the dim light cast by the fire, though, I could see his jaw clench.

"Keep watching, baby. I want you to just sit there while I fuck your friend until I feel him come deep inside me." She took my cock in her hand, placed it against her pussy, and sank down on me before I realized what was happening.

Everything about Amber felt so different. Good, but different. Her scent. The way she moved on me. The press of her tits. The aggressive way she kissed me.

Drawing back, I think she came to the same conclusion that I had: we were not fucking our partners. The game fell away. The questions, the fantasies, fell away under the intensity of that raw intimacy. We were back to those two intense weeks when we were a couple, sharing a moment.

Fear, uncertainty, anxiety—I saw them darken her face. Our collective unconscious asked the question together: Was this happening? Was this really fucking happening?

I nodded, answering for us both. *We're going to be okay. This feels so right.*

And then we were fucking again.

"So how does it feel to watch them, Paul?" Beth teased. "Is the reality as good as the fantasy?"

Paul didn't respond. He never even looked at Beth. All attention was on Amber as she undulated in my lap.

"That's it, Jason," Beth said. "Show them how good you are. God, that's hot."

I grabbed Amber's ass, guiding her along my length. Unlike when I was with Beth, Amber fought the help, bucking harder like this was some kind of competition. Who could fuck fastest? Who could get off first?

Amber was moaning like she thought it would be her. "Yeah, yeah!"

I didn't mind. In fact, if anything, I wanted to give her what she wanted. I wanted to blow her mind. I attacked her neck with my mouth, nibbling along that tall column of sweaty flesh. Her blood raced beneath my lips. I felt it thud and thrive, just below the surface.

She moaned, thrusting her chest up and out, burying me between her tits. I adjusted, finding her nipple and flicking it with my tongue. She pressed harder, filling my mouth with tit-flesh. Her hips were wild in my lap—I let her do her thing, my hands on her ass only to keep her from popping off me.

"Yes, Jason. Yes." Her voice was tight. Clipped. Like she was fighting for each word. "Fuck. Right there!"

When my teeth grazed her nipple, it was like touching a match to pool of gasoline. Amber's fingers seized in my hair as she came. I could *feel*—more than hear—her orgasm. Could feel it thrum deep inside of her, the nucleus of a bomb seconds before it washed over me.

"Oh, Jason! Oh! Jason!" She shouted my name with each thundering drive down my cock. My head went light. I nearly joined her. Nearly released myself into her singing depths. Something told me to wait—said, *Easy...easy...*

Behind Amber, I heard Beth whispering, but it took me a moment to hear what she was saying. Or where she was.

"He's going to come inside her," Beth said. "I bet she didn't ask for your permission, either. Did she? I know Jason didn't…"

Something was off. Her voice wasn't coming from my right. I looked. Only Casey was there, her eyes fixed not on me and Amber, but something on the other couch.

Beth went on. "She just went for it, without stopping even once to ask. To check on you."

I found Beth snuggled against Paul on the loveseat. She was naked, as was Paul, and had her hand wrapped around Paul's thick erection. She was whispering into his ear, loud enough for me to hear, but intimate enough to send a shiver up my spine.

She looked across at me. "She should have asked, right? As a good girlfriend, she should have asked. Something like, *Hey, Jason, mind if I suck Paul's cock?*"

My chest tightened. Fire raced along my scalp. She was asking. She was getting my permission. I could barely breathe. Couldn't talk. So I nodded. I nodded my fucking head and let this happen.

Beth smiled. "See? Just like that."

My wife lowered her head into Paul's lap, held his cock steady, and wrapped her mouth around the head.

"Ohmygod!" It took me a moment to realize that moan was my own, and by that time, I was filling another woman with my come.

That triggered a second climax in Amber, who clutched me to her shoulder and heaved through her release. She felt great—yet I barely noticed past the gut-wrenching sight of Beth as she slid her lips along another man's cock. I knew exactly what he was feeling—knew the way she worked her hand in unison, knew how she sucked as she pulled off, and how her tongue felt like it was somehow swirling around the entirety of it. I'd watched her do this countless times—just never from this angle.

"Jesus," Paul cried. He tried her to pull her away—at first, I thought, out of fear. Then I saw the way his breath caught and his jaw set. I saw that telltale tightness in his face before he erupted inside Beth's mouth.

Casey, beside me, joined the rest of us. She'd been furiously playing with herself as she watched. Both hands worked her pussy, one to expose her clit, the other to tease out her orgasm—or that's what I think I saw in the half-second I spent looking. Any other time, the sight of the sexy brunette jerking off would have me mesmerized.

Any other time that didn't involve my Beth swallowing another man's come.

Amber came down from her high in time to see what was happening behind her—to see what our partners were up to. I held my breath for moment, worried that she'd cause a scene. Instead, she said, "God, that's sexy."

She was so quiet that I didn't think she meant it for me, but I answered her like she had.

"Glad you're not going to cut his balls off."

Amber looked back at me, the sass back in her face. I was still buried inside her, despite growing soft. It felt good. Comfortable. She wrapped her arms around me and drew close without kissing me. "Oh, she asked me if it was okay earlier."

Paul's voice croaked as he asked his question. "So this was all planned?"

"I mean, you can't really plan something like this." Beth grabbed a glass of wine off the coffee table and finished it off. "But after listening to everyone confess their fantasies, I kind of wanted you guys to experience them."

Paul looked at the rest of us, more bewildered than upset. "And you all knew about this?"

I wondered the same thing. I knew, of course—or a part of it, anyway—and apparently so did Amber. Did Casey?

Amber responded to Paul, and not for the first time, I worried that this would all come crashing down. "Don't get all uptight now. You just got a blowjob from my best friend and didn't seem to be complaining."

"That was—"

"And don't tell me it didn't get you excited to watch me fuck Jason. You've brought it up enough in the last month."

"Amber…" Paul looked horrified that this was all coming up. He licked his lips, trying to make up his mind whether to get angry or not.

Amber hugged me close, staring at Paul over her shoulder. "Mmm, I can feel his come inside me. Makes me feel so naughty."

"Amber…"

"Paul." Amber laughed. "Now that I know you can handle it, the next time some guy hits on me and I'm attracted to him, I'm going to make sure I get his number. It's been forever since I've been on a date."

Paul squirmed. He was getting hard again, and since he was naked, he couldn't hide it. I waited for him to explode. For Paul to do what he always did—to storm off, or hit someone. To flex his masculinity. His eyes went from Amber's to mine to Amber's. He seemed to come to some conclusion.

Standing, he grabbed a beer and held his hand out to Beth. "Well, if we're fulfilling fantasies, want to do mine?"

My stomach squirmed. Beth looked at me, our eyes meeting. We had a whole conversation in that look.

I don't have to…

No, I trust you.

You sure?

The unspoken question coiled around my chest, squeezing the air out of me. Our safe word sprang to mind. *Apples and oranges.* A way out. A way to stop this madness. I almost said it. I could practically feel the words form on my tongue. But I didn't.

Turned out, the hardest thing for me to say that evening was also the hottest: "Have fun you two. See you in the morning."

I watched Paul and Beth make their way up the stairs, naked

and ready to fuck. Paul wasn't even fully erect and he was already bigger than me. *Fuck, was this a good idea?*

I didn't realize I'd started to stiffen inside Amber until she looked at me in surprise. "Ready for round three already?"

"Almost."

"Someone likes the idea of a naughty wife as much as Paul likes a naughty girlfriend. Hey Case, want to go up to Jason's bedroom? I think we need to put on a show..."

Chapter 10:
Threesome

I don't remember climbing onto the bed. I don't even remember moving into the bedroom. Between what had just happened in the living room and the idea that just down the hall, Beth was getting plowed by my best friend, my mind wasn't on the present.

Insecurity throttled me. Beth hadn't gone upstairs with Paul out of duty to her cause—she wasn't fucking him just to fulfill his fantasy. She wanted it, too. Was she curious about experiencing a cock so big? Would she be getting something that I couldn't give her?

Amber's voice returned me to the present. "Hey, Jace, remember back when we were dating and you told me how much you really wanted to have a threesome?"

"Huh?"

It was like I realized Amber was there for the first time, even though I'm positive I'd followed her cute ass up the stairs.

"You remember what I told you? That I don't swing that way?"

The scene came into focus and thoughts of Beth fled, along with my insecurities. Amber was sitting at the foot of the bed, somehow looking gracefully modest despite her nudity. Casey stood behind her, a smile stretched across her elfin face.

"I remember now. Yeah. You shot me down so fast that I never mentioned that fantasy to anyone again."

"So you've never had a threesome?" Amber asked. "That fantasy is unfulfilled?"

My cock reacted to the implication. I just nodded.

Amber turned to Casey, reaching up to draw her into her lap. "So earlier, when you said that you were most attracted to me…"

"I was being honest," Casey finished. She brushed a strand of golden hair from Amber's eyes. The two of them seemed to turn to give me the perfect profile of their faces. "You are one of the most beautiful women I've ever met."

"Means a lot, coming from someone as attractive as you," Amber said.

"But you don't swing that way." Casey giggled.

"I didn't…back then."

"Good to know." Casey closed the gap, kissing Amber before the blonde lost her nerve.

I will never tire of watching two sexy women make out. I loved the way they pushed their long hair from their faces as they melted into each other. I loved how their curves complimented one another, a yin-yang of soft female flesh.

Casey kissed Amber softly at first just lips to lips. She alternated her kisses, tilting her head left, then right, then left again, checking on the blonde between each kiss. Amber's eyes remained closed, ready for the next touch. When Casey pushing her tongue into her mouth, she accepted it willingly, her own tongue unrolling to greet it.

I'd watched Amber and Beth kiss earlier, then Beth and Casey. This was hotter than both. That image seared into my brain: lines being crossed, innocence being left at the door—if you could call Amber innocent at all. When Casey pulled back and looked into Amber's eyes, we all heard the question.

You ready for this?

Amber nodded, ever so slightly. I saw her blush. Saw the way she looked over at me, reminding herself that she wasn't alone.

Casey licked her lips and slid out of Amber's lap. She leaned Amber back and moved down between the blonde's legs. Amber reached out for my hand and I took it, squeezing it to give her courage.

She moaned, stiffening as Casey dipped her head between Amber's thighs and ran her tongue across Amber's bare shaven mound.

Casey looked up. "I can taste Jason inside you. That's so hot."

"Oh, my God," Amber moaned as Casey's mouth returned to her pussy. From my angle, I could see every lurid detail. Casey curled her tongue along Amber's slit, pushing it deep before dragging it up and across her engorged button. I could see the white film of my come as Casey cleaned her out.

Amber squeezed my hand harder, pulling close. I leaned in and kissed her as best I could as she gasped and moaned.

"She...she...ah..."

"Shh...just enjoy it," I said. I kissed down her chest, filling my hands with her soft tits. "Know what I'm going to enjoy most? Fucking you while you eat Casey."

I sucked on her nipples and felt them respond in my mouth, growing hard and long. If memory served me, Amber could come from playing with her nipples alone. Between me and Casey, she didn't have a chance.

"Oh, my gaw... She's got her fin—gah! Fingers in me..." Amber bucked beneath me, jutting her chest into my mouth as she let loose a shrieking moan.

I didn't relent, lashing those hard nipples as she rode out her orgasm. Casey pulled back, sitting on her ankles to watch Amber crest.

She had the look of pure satisfaction—a job well done.

Then she looked at me. Her next challenge?

I sat back against the sloping pillows piled at the head of the bed and met Casey's gaze.

"So Jason..." I'd never thought of Casey's voice as husky, but that's all I could think about as she crawled up onto the bed. "You know Beth let us in on her plans, right?"

"I'm starting to piece that together, yeah."

"And since you never told us what any of *your* fantasies were, she filled us in."

"Oh? What does Beth think my fantasies are?"

Casey crawled over to me, a miracle of curves squeezed into a tight body. I didn't reach out and touch her, even though I wanted to. She had a boyfriend. She was off limits.

"A threesome with two girls, of course." Casey looked at Amber, who was still recovering. "We'll get back to that soon."

"We wore her out, didn't we?"

Casey smiled. "She's got a body built for fucking. She'll be ready again."

"Did Beth tell you any other fantasies of mine?"

"There was one other..." Casey rose up onto her knees, working her way into a straddle over my legs. I had an uninstructed view of her naked body. It was a thing of glory She was voluptuous while being slender with hips that flared and tits that were too good to be true.

"You like what you see, Jason?"

"Of course, but we can't, Case—"

"Do you want to fuck me?" She draped herself over my reclined body, pressing her warm tits against me. Leaning close enough to kiss, she asked, "Because I *really* want to fuck *you*."

She reached between us, guiding my cock against her bald, slippery pussy. I groaned. She felt so slick. So wet.

"But here's the one condition," she said. She produced her phone, holding it between us. "I'm going to have to share this with my boyfriend. That's the deal."

"Share?"

"Here. Let me show you." Loading up the camera app, she leaned back enough to point the camera between us and took a photo of the way she was grinding on my shaft. "That's not great, but you get the idea. Now take this."

As I took it, she rose off me and guided me onto my back. Wrapping a hand around my cock, she said, "Flip it to video, would you?"

"I don't know about this, Case."

"Oh yeah?" She dipped forward, licking her way down my shaft and across my balls. She swallowed them one after another, rolling them swiftly before releasing me. The sensation ripped a moan from me, taking me completely by surprise. "Sounds like you're pretty sure about what you want. Now flip it to video."

I shivered and did as I was told.

"We live?"

I nodded, pointing her phone at her face and my cock.

"Hey, baby," Casey said into the camera. "As you can see, I'm being a little naughty. I tried so hard to be good, but...well, the temptation was too great. I've already fooled around with the two girls, and that was fun, but right now I need to feel a stiff, hard cock inside me. Luckily, Jason here is being more than accommodating."

She swallowed my shaft, giving it a couple quick bobs before noisily pulling away.

"He's so hard. Fuck, this is going to feel good."

With that, she rose over me. I kept the picture on my cock as she positioned it against her bald cunt. Seeing it on that little screen reinforced how obscene this was. She sank down enough to take my cockhead into her swollen lips. I'd never watched myself so close up.

Casey groaned as I split her, keeping the narrative up, her voice strained. "It feels so...so fucking good. So...different."

She spread herself open with her fingers as she sank lower, leaving nothing to the imagination. I watched us cross the line through the screen of the phone, even though I could have watched the real thing.

"There." The word became multisyllabic as she sank all the way to my root. "There," she repeated in a whisper.

I shut the video recorder off and tossed it beside me. "We done with the documentary?"

Casey giggled, although that quickly gave way to a gasp as I pushed up off the mattress. She rose over me, undulating her hips as we fell into a slow, steady rhythm. Her breathing came unsteadily, hitching and sputtering as we fucked.

"So is this something you do regularly?" I asked, looking at the phone by my side.

"Ha…" It was half a laugh, mostly a sigh. "No. First time. But we have an understanding…"

"Like an open relationship?"

"Stop trying to categorize it, Jace." Casey bent over me, brushing her lips along mine. "Do you consider yourself in an open relationship? 'Cause Beth's fucking Paul right now."

Casey's eyes grew wide as she felt my visceral reaction. For a moment, I'd forgotten about Beth in the other room—Beth having sex with another man.

"Makes you jealous, doesn't it?" Casey asked. She didn't draw away, her face still inches from my own, but she did start to fuck me faster. "Think he's made her come yet? Think she's gotten off fucking Paul's big cock?"

"Fuck, Casey," I moaned.

"That's a start." She kissed me hard, jamming her tongue down my throat as she fucked me. There was no mistaking that I was with someone else.

Casey was tighter than Beth. More compact. I could feel her glasses against my face as we kissed. And the way she fucked me was so much more possessive. She took me, and she took me hard. Even when she rolled us, putting me on top, I knew who was really in control.

"Fuck me, Jason." She wrapped her legs around my back, guiding my thrusts. "Think of your wife getting fucked out there. Think of how he must be making her moan. Feel that adrenaline? Use it on me."

I did. I lunged. I pounded. I felt the veins in my neck pulse and my biceps quiver.

"Fuck me! Yes! Like that!"

I could just hear her over the roar of blood.

I fucked her the way I thought Paul would be fucking my wife—the way I *wanted* Paul to fuck my wife. I brought new meaning to the term *to take*. I took and took and took. I took everything I could from her. She ran her fingernails across my back. I dug my toes into the mattress so I could thrust that much harder.

Her body buckled back. I didn't stop thrusting. She wanted relentlessness. She'd get it.

I nibbled at her collarbone, tasting the salt of her sweat. I licked along her exposed neck, feeling her pulse beat a rapid staccato. Her life blood.

"Uh, God, Jace! Fuck me. Fuck. Me!"

Casey was there. She'd arrived, crashing and thrashing through her orgasm. I wanted to join—would have had it not been for those two previous orgasms. Instead, I took pleasure in the quivering feel of her climax around my cock and the ragged breathing I'd reduced her to.

Her legs relaxed on me, fell to either side. She put a hand on her forehead but didn't open her eyes.

"That was incredible," Amber said.

Amber. Right. We had an audience. Looking over, the first thing I noticed was that she had Casey's phone held out in her hand, filming us. The next was that her free hand was buried between her legs.

"I want you to fuck me like you just fucked her," she said.

"How about I fuck you both?"

Amber looked at me funny. I got off of Casey—moaning as I pulled free of her pussy. "Ladies first."

Amber picked up on what I wanted quickly. Straddling Casey, pussy against pussy, tits against tits, she bent low and kissed the other woman.

Casey stirred, welcoming the Sapphic kiss. I watched them make out, watched their languid movements grow more energized. Casey planted her feet into the mattress, pushing her hips up into Amber's. Amber shifted, driving her bare mound against Casey's, skin meeting skin, clit rubbing against clit.

Amber broke the kiss and looked over her shoulder at me, raising an eyebrow. *Ready?*

I was. Cock in hand, I took my place between their legs, steadied myself on Amber's back, and eased into her soaking pussy. Sinking all the way in, my balls came to rest on Casey's equally wet cunt.

"God, that feels good," I blurted.

Amber moaned. "You have no idea."

I stroked her gently at first, getting used to the angle—falling in love with the slippery welcome that came with each push. The mews of not one but two women beneath me spurred me on. I braced myself on Casey's knees as I started fucking Amber faster. Athletically, Casey kept her pussy pressed hard against Amber's, lifting her ass as my balls clapped against her clit with each thrust.

Without warning, I switched, pulling free of Amber and sinking into Casey's primed womanhood.

The difference in their pussies was subtle, yet profound. Casey was tight where Amber was deep; Casey was compact, gripping me with each stroke, while Amber's embrace was sleek and scintillating. Dipping back and forth, I tried to make up my mind which felt better. In the end, I couldn't decide; like the women beneath me, I loved them both.

Our threesome moaned and gasped, closing in on a collective orgasm. The girls kissed when they could, but mostly just clung to one another as we fucked.

"I can feel him in you," Casey whispered to Amber. "Your clit feels so fucking big against me when he's there."

Amber's response was a jumbled mess, a moan that became a gasp that became a cry. I fucked her harder, deep strokes that bottomed out inside her and drove my balls against Casey's pussy.

"I want his come," Casey said. "You already got it. I want it next."

"Okay," Amber cried, her voice cracking.

Testosterone flood my veins. They didn't get to determine that. *I* did. I was in control. I was the one fucking them. I switched back to Amber, intending to prove them wrong. Intending to empty my second deposit inside my one-time lover's pussy.

I started to tell them. Casey didn't call the shots. And then, Casey whispered into Amber's ear and I nearly came.

"And when he comes inside me, I want you to eat it out of me."

"Uh, God!" Amber cried. Her pussy rippled around my cock, milking it as she came. I clenched my teeth and fought the temptation to just give it to her.

Paradoxically, the image of Amber going down on Casey gave me the will to hold back. I switched out of Amber, my cockhead gliding across the slick union of their pussies. As I slotted myself one last time inside Casey, I felt that scrap of willpower go. I fucked her once. Twice. And then I was gone.

Casey bucked up, grinding against me, against Amber, against the decadence of the moment. She seized the bed sheets around us, crying out, brow furrowed, until Amber cut her off with a kiss.

I pulled away, first to my haunches, then all the way on to my back. I was done. Three times and I was out. TKO, baby.

I vaguely recalled watching Amber slip beneath the sheets, down between Casey's legs. I have the distinct vision of Casey's fingers raking through Amber's golden hair as she went to work.

I wanted to keep watching. I fought off the fatigue, but in the end, it got me. In the end, I crashed into inky, delirious sleep.

Chapter 11:
The Morning After

Waking up between two naked, sleeping women left me disoriented. After opening my eyes to Beth every morning for the last three years, I nearly shot out of bed at the wrongness of the situation. I was spooning Casey's petite body with Amber behind me, her full tits pressed into my back.

I was hard, and after last night, being hard was painful.

I took a couple deep breaths, fighting for calm. I hadn't been with anyone else since I'd started dating Beth. Long before I watched her walk down that aisle, I figured I never would. That prospect never scared me. Never made me feel trapped. Yet now, I was sandwiched between two really attractive women who I most definitely had fucked last night.

I slowly extracted myself from between their bodies. They shifted, but neither woke up. I fought off the cold, along with my bewildered emotions. Guilt was in there—but so was excitement and shock. Holy shit, I'd fucked Casey and Amber? I'd watched them fuck each other?

As I grabbed my robe and slipped out into the hall, another

realization shook my core. Beth hadn't returned to our room. She didn't give me much time to wonder where she was, either.

"Ah! AH!" The unmistakable sounds of Beth in the throes of passion filtered down the hall.

Something warm and fuzzy twisted in my gut. I felt vertigo, grabbing at the walls as images of what was happening—what had happened all night long?—came crashing in. I don't remember approaching the door, but suddenly I was in front of it, the sounds of sex clear through the flimsy wood.

"You like that?" I heard Paul grunt. "You like the way my cock feels inside of you?"

"Yes," she whispered. Then, shouting, "Yes!"

"Say it," Paul demanded. "Tell me you love how good this feels."

I held my breath. My heart beat like a trapped animal against my chest. I waited for her to say it. To admit something that I wanted to hear, but didn't.

Instead, Beth laughed. It was a strained laugh—one delivered through intense pleasure—but it was also unmistakably Beth. "Can't you just fuck me? Why do men always have to let their egos get in the way?"

I smiled, relaxing.

Paul shot back. "Says the chick who woke me up with a blowjob."

"Well, it was driving into my hip like a fucking baseball bat. What else was I supposed to do with it?"

The jealousy I felt was easier to deal with. Beth didn't even know I was there and she was saying all the right things.

"Besides," she went on. "Doesn't it take a *real man* to keep up with two horny nymphos at once? You know, Amber looked pretty pleased when she fucked Jason. I've never seen her come like that."

I heard them shift—heard them kiss. The grunting returned.

Paul said, "You're going to play that game, huh?"

"Yeah. Fuck me, Paul. Fuck me like you hope Jason fucked Amber all night long."

"You're a dirty whore."

Beth's reply was strained. "No, babe. That's your girlfriend."

"Fuck you. Fuck...you!"

After last night, there was no risk of me coming with them, but my dick was hard enough that I could have tried. I nearly moaned as I listened to Beth crash through another loud orgasm—this time arriving as Paul filled her with his come.

I considering barging in. I considering joining them. Instead, I headed downstairs. I needed to get my head on straight, and I needed a break from sex. At least for a couple more hours.

When I got downstairs, things felt bright—and it wasn't just the sun reflecting off a wasteland of white around the house. I stood at the window and surveyed the glacial landscape. It was like someone had pressed the pause button on the world. Everything was stuck.

Yet that scene wasn't what brightened my world. That belonged to Beth. It always would. Even as she got thoroughly fucked by my best friend upstairs, she held true to me. And when this snow had melted away enough to end this crazy few days, we'd be together again—the couple that pledged *'til death do us part.*

I set the coffee maker to brew a full pot, finished off the bowl of pasta salad in the fridge, and decided to tackle the snow outside.

A neighbor had plowed our long, tree-lined driveway, but the turnaround was still piled high with over a foot of snow. It was warmer than it had been yesterday and with the sun out, our house guests could probably leave sooner rather than later now.

The thought was bitter-sweet. I liked having them around—it felt like camp for adults, if you left out the sex part—but I wanted my life back. And I needed some time with Beth, just the two of us.

"Digging us out of your life?" Paul asked, startling me from my thoughts. I'd done about a third of what was needed to get his SUV out, just didn't realize that's what I'd been doing.

"Can't wait to send you on your way."

"Seems like a good idea. Before your wife gets *too* addicted to my cock," Paul said.

My fist flashed out before I realized I wanted to punch him. My knuckles crunched into his square jaw. Pain shot up my arm.

Paul reeled back, clutching his face. He spit into the snow, staining it red with bloody spittle. He'd lost his hat and his styled, blonde hair was mussed. For a moment, he was the bull, with eyes that flashed bloody murder and nostrils that flared and snorted. I thought he was going to come at me. Paul had height and mass on me. If he wanted to kick my ass, he could.

Then he relaxed his shoulders and did something I'd only seen him do a couple times in his life. He said, "I'm sorry, man."

"You're an asshole." The adrenaline hadn't quite left me.

"It's a defense mechanism."

"I know," I said. "I should be used to it."

Paul tested his jaw, rubbing the red spot where I'd connected. "Feel better?" he asked.

"A little. But you're still an asshole."

He grinned. "Want a beer?"

"It's like 9:30 in the morning," I said. Paul just stared, so I shrugged. "Love one."

We circled the house to the porch so we wouldn't have to worry about tracking snow in. I said, "So about last night..."

"Pretty crazy, huh? Don't hit me again, but Beth is amazing in bed."

"Ditto for Amber."

"And Case?"

"The nerdy girl's probably the wildest of us all."

We got to the keg. He pumped, I poured, and we wandered over to the patio furniture. I sank into the plush snow and sipped the ice cold drink.

"I wouldn't have done it if I knew you didn't want me to, you know," I said.

Paul laughed. "Amber wasn't giving you much choice."

"There's always a choice."

Paul nodded. "I know you wouldn't have. And I'd be lying if I told you it wasn't exciting to watch." He drained his beer and stood to get another. "It's all fucked up."

"I know what you mean. I heard you two this morning, you know. It was...it was really hot."

We drank. It was quiet out here. Muffled. Occasionally, I'd hear the soft whoosh of snow sliding off a tree branch. Nothing more.

The door slid open, warm air buffeting us as we were joined by a third.

"Morning, Case," Paul said. "You get any sleep?"

"When your girlfriend let me." She winked. "For someone who says she's never been with another woman, Amber sure can eat pussy."

"She...you...?" Paul's jaw dropped. He looked at me for confirmation. I nodded.

Casey giggled. "Did we have sex? Oh yes, more than once. In fact, we just had some fun in the shower. I can still feel her mouth on me. Mmm..."

"That's insane."

"Everything about last night was." Casey went over to the keg. The nozzle hissed when her cup was half full. "Looks like this thing is finally kicked. What happened to it lasting a week?"

Paul laughed. "Guess we can drink enough for a whole party."

"We're getting low on a lot of things," I added.

"Jason's ready for us to leave."

Casey smirked. "Maybe you, but I doubt he's ready for me and Amber to go. You should have seen him last night. Incredible."

I actually blushed at that.

"Remember Europe?" Casey asked.

"How could I forget?" Paul said. "I planned the whole damn thing."

In the summer between high school and college, the three of us decided to backpack around Europe—our last hurrah before we all went our separate ways.

Casey went on. "You guys were so set on going—and me coming along—that I never had much of a chance to stop and think about what the hell we were doing."

"I think we all felt that way," I said. "I remember getting on the train heading to some new city—Prague or Budapest or whatever—and having no idea where we'd sleep that night."

"But it was thrilling, right?" Casey asked.

"One of the best times of my life."

"Kind of like now, huh?" Casey paused, letting us make the connections.

She was right. Everything about these past few days was crazy, uncertain, but in the end, more fun than I could ever have imagined.

Casey continued. "And you know what? We're better people for that trip. We know ourselves better. I don't think college would have been the same had I not gotten drunk in some village in Austria, stumbled home, and vomited in my hostel bed."

Paul cleared his throat. "I believe that was my bed."

Casey smiled. "That's right."

"So you're saying group sex and swinging is equivalent to backpacking across Europe?" I asked.

"I'm saying that we should never stop seeking that adventure. I've been thinking a lot about it since Vegas. Life's too hard to plan everything out. Take the adventure as it's presented. You won't regret it."

"Spoken like someone totally single," I said.

"Hey, I have a boyfriend!"

"Mostly single, then. I'm just saying that while you're right—we need to remember that *fun is a state of mind* and all that—we also need to remember that we're in this with someone else."

I looked toward the house, where Beth was busy doing whatever she did after fucking another guy all night—sleeping or showering were my guesses. I felt the tug to join her, to be with her.

I stood, brushing snow off my pants. "Sounds like you've got a really understanding, cool guy now. My advice would be to keep communicating—even when you don't think you need to. Now, time for me to do as I say. See you in there."

****

I found Beth in the kitchen, alone with a bowl of cereal and a couple slices of toast. She'd dressed already, putting on a beige cable knit sweater and a pair of tight jeans. It was the facade of the girl-next-door. Did I believe it anymore?

"Morning." Beth's voice was a little rough around the edges. From moaning all night? Or just from lack of sleep?

I shifted at the uncomfortable questions. "Morning."

I sat down beside her, taking her hands in mine. She didn't have bags under her eyes, although I detected the faint sparkle of concealer there. When she looked at me, all I saw was the bright, vibrant woman I'd fallen in love with.

"You have fun last night?" I said.

Beth looked away briefly, color mixing in with her freckles. "Yes."

"I know. I heard some of that."

"You heard?"

"This morning. Sounded like you didn't get much rest. I was on my way down, and heard you two."

The color in Beth's face deepened. "I'm sorry."

"Why? It was...amazing to hear," I said. "Last night, when you saw me with Amber, did it upset you?"

"Nope. It was as hot as I'd imagined it. I mean, I got a little jealous, but I expected that. It was cool because I knew exactly how she was feeling. I recognized your moves—like some personalized porn shoot or something." Her expression turned serious. "But it was different with me and Paul. You didn't get to watch. I...I shouldn't have let him lead me away like that."

"Hey, no, it's cool." I squeezed her hands, tracing the diamond on her engagement ring.

"No, it's not. We didn't discuss that." Tears began to form in Beth's eyes.

I scooted my chair closer and put an arm around her. "Hey, Beth, I promise, it's okay."

Beth smiled. A tear pulled loose, sliding across her cheek. "I got caught up in the moment."

"You got caught up in the idea of Paul's super cock, you mean."

"No, of course not," she said quickly. When she saw my frank expression, she sighed. "Okay, maybe that had something to do with it."

"Honestly, was he better than me?" I winced at how that sounded.

"No, not even close." She wiped the remnants of her tears away and snuggled into me. "He was different, of course, and he knows what he's doing. But what you and I have...I've never had that with anyone else."

I thought of the wild sex I'd just had last night with Amber and Casey. "I know exactly what you mean."

"So I ran into Casey after the shower. Sounds like you three had a good time, too. So you fucked them at the same time, huh?"

My turn to blush. "Yeah. It just sort of happened."

Beth let out a laugh, clear and heart-warming. "That's sort of the motto of the weekend, isn't it? *It just sort of happened.*"

"And you're still not mad? Or hurt? Or at all upset?"

"I'm not. Not mad, anyway. Definitely not hurt. Makes me a little jealous if I'm honest, but also really turned on." She twisted to face me, running her hands up my chest with a sigh. "You're so sexy, baby. Thinking of you keeping up with Casey and Amber is so fucking hot."

She kissed me, our bottled emotions spilling forth as our tongues lashed. I felt her hand cup my crotch, finding me hard.

Beth drew back, her lips hovering close. "It makes me proud of you, as fucked up as that sounds. Makes me excited to know that I married a man who can make those two sluts beg for it."

I wanted to take her right there on the kitchen table. The kissing didn't help. But Beth shifted back to hostess mode before I could get us there.

"We need to think about lunch. The leftovers from the party are pretty much done."

"Keg's empty, too."

Beth laughed. "Of course you'd know that. I was thinking that we cook up a big batch of pasta. Do spaghetti carbonara or something. After last night, we could all use some carbs."

"Someone came through and plowed the driveway. We could probably get to the store."

Beth hesitated. "We could..."

"Yeah, I feel the same way. Stay disconnected from it all. At least for one more day."

"One more day," she agreed.

"Besides, we've done everyone's fantasy but yours."

Beth grinned. "I didn't say it. So you're sure you're okay with it?"

"If I can handle you spending the night with Paul, I think I've proven that I'm okay with sharing you."

"Fair enough."

"Actually, I'm looking forward to it. My one regret last night was that I didn't get to see you in action."

"Well, let's start on that carb-filled lunch. I think we're all going to need it."

****

We had lunch. I showered. Paul showered. Casey spent a long time on the phone with her boyfriend, coming out flushed yet quiet.

We watched the news. Temperatures were on the rise. Streets were getting plowed. The government wasn't immediately closed down tomorrow. This was probably our last day as a group, and we all knew what that meant: this game that we'd begun had one final hurrah.

We all kept waiting for someone else to make the first move. We played video games. We read. We grazed in the kitchen. The house buzzed with nervous energy—metaphorical virgins on the metaphorical night before prom.

Of course, that didn't stop Beth from teasing me every chance she got.

Things like, "I'm wearing that lacy black bra and thong you got me for my birthday last year. Think Paul's going to like it?"

Or, "Paul prefers his women clean shaven. Maybe I should try the look."

Or, "I can't wait to feel Paul's hot come fill me up. Again. So naughty."

She'd whisper the teases, give me a quick kiss, then saunter off before I could come up with a response.

Amber and Casey were no better, although they were not quite so obvious. Amber wore her black yoga pants and a long, tight sweater that she'd borrowed from Beth. It looked good on my wife, but Amber filled it out like it was designed to be. Casey wore a sweaterdress over her skin-tight jeans, tight and short enough to make me wish she didn't have the jeans.

They seemed to revel in the taunting. Casey made sure to flash those tits at me with a smile every chance she got. Amber was actually more subtle, staring at me a beat too long, touching her hair like she harbored a crush.

Amber and I ended up chatting as I fed new logs into the fire.

"How do you and Beth do it?" she asked.

"Well, we normally like to be naked in bed—although she sometimes wears some lacy lingerie—and we start with kissing—"

"Stop, you goof. You know what I mean. You two are so happy together. I could swear you'd just gotten married sometimes. The way she looks at you, or you at her." Amber shook her head. "I'm envious."

I wasn't sure what to say to that. I was supposed to be seducing her, not having a conversation about the strengths of my marriage. "You and Paul look like that, too."

"Please." She glanced into the fire, where the new logs were catching. "Paul and I are good, but...I don't know. If we were *really* good, we wouldn't be talking about other guys."

"But that turns you on, too, right?"

She sighed. "Yeah. I'm not saying this is all on Paul. That's just it. It's my fantasy, too."

"And that makes you feel guilty."

"It does." She looked at me, firelight dancing across her striking features: her cheekbones, her nose, her high forehead and perfectly groomed eyebrows. "I guess I never got all that out of my system back in college. Not like Casey or Beth—"

"Doesn't seem like it's totally out of Casey's."

Amber released a begrudging laugh. "No. But she's also single..."

"As single as you. She's got a boyfriend, too."

"Anyway, my point is, sometimes I think about what it would be like, being with other men. Like that guy at the bar, Andrew. I'd be lying if I told you that I wasn't tempted. But I still love Paul. I want to marry him. I want to spend my life with him."

"So you're having a hard time linking those feelings up with the other ones."

"Right! How can I want Paul, and also want to get picked up in a bar by a stranger and get fucked in the bathroom?"

My cock stirred at that thought. I stuck with the Good Friend Routine. "But here's the thing you're missing, Amb. Paul also wants you to have those experiences. He gets off on them."

"And is that something to build a marriage on?"

"Stop being so conventional. What we're talking about in broader terms is honesty. You two have these fantasies; it's better to talk about them openly rather than harbor them in secret."

I let her chew on that thought for a moment.

"You asked me how Beth and I do it. *That's* how. We're open and honest with each other. We don't let things fester. If either of us has a problem, we tell the other."

Amber cracked a smile. "So neither of you had a problem with last night?"

Her smile was infectious. "Nothing that'd qualify as a *problem.*

There was some jealousy, sure, but we worked through it. And we trust each other."

Amber leaned forward and kissed me softly on the lips. "You two are still a wonder. I'm happy to have you guys as friends."

"Eh hem." Beth cleared her throat from the doorway from the den, startling the two of us. Behind her stood Paul, his expression blank. Turning back to Paul, Beth said, "See, can't leave those two alone for five minutes before they're all over each other."

"Hey, it's not like that—" Amber began.

Paul hugged Beth against him. "Two can play at that game."

Beth turned in his arms and rocked her head back to accept his kiss. I gasped. I couldn't breathe. Beth pushed her tongue past Paul's lips. Paul's hands went to her ass, squeezing them through her tight jeans.

I felt Amber's hand clutch at my thigh, just above my knee. She shifted beside me. Her eyes were wide, barely blinking.

"Are you okay?" I whispered.

Amber snapped out of her trance and glanced at me. "I'm good. Horny, though."

Casey's voice boomed out from the top of the stairs. "Okay, y'all. Everything's set up here."

Beth and Paul detached. I looked quizzically at Amber. The blonde smiled and shook her head: *I'm not telling.* Instead, she stood and offered her hand to me.

"Come on. We've got a little surprise for you boys."

Beth and Amber led us upstairs, where Casey was waiting by the door to the master bedroom. I could smell the burning wax of candles. Beyond, the room flickered and danced with their pale light.

The room was filled with every candle we had in the house. The bed was made up in the black satin sheets that someone had given us as a gag gift that we never got rid of. Pillows were stacked along the headboard.

On either side of the bed, facing each other, were chairs from our dining set—the chairs designed to sit at the heads, replete with cushioned arms. Piled in each chair were a tangle of my neck ties.

"Gentleman," Casey said, "Please take your seats."

Chapter 12:
Beth's Fantasy

Beth led me over to my chair, sitting me down as Amber did the same for Paul. I gave Beth a look that I hoped asked, *What's going on here?* She just smiled, shook her head ever so slightly, and reached for the bundle of ties.

Paul wasn't as quiet. "Amb, you know I'm not into this shit."

"Hmm…I'm not so sure about that." The blonde yanked the tie holding his wrist tight and knotted it off. "You pretend to like being in control, but I think that deep down, you like giving it up even more."

He looked ready to fire back, but didn't stop her from tying down his other wrist. Casey floated over, tying his legs to the chair before checking his restraints.

"He good?" Amber asked.

"He's not going anywhere," Casey nodded.

Amber grinned, standing tall. "Enjoy the show."

Casey and Beth finishing tying me to the chair before Beth blew me a kiss. The three women disappeared out of the room.

"Do you know what the hell's going on?" Paul asked. He tugged at his restraints.

"No idea, but I have a feeling we're going to like it."

We sat in silence for a couple minutes before Paul spoke. "So what was your fantasy?"

"I'm sorry?"

"*Your fantasy.* Beth's been fulfilling our fantasies. Case got to watch. Amber got her fling. I got your wife." He grinned. "So what was yours?"

"Everyone keeps asking me that. I really don't know. This whole weekend has been pretty great."

"What do you want, man? This is your chance."

"Well, I kind of had a lot of them done to me last night, but if you really want to know...I think it would be really hot to watch Beth and Amber get it on."

"Totally. I'm a little jealous that you got to watch Amb hook up with her first chick last night."

"You'll probably get a taste of that in a few."

"I hope so," Paul said.

Silence descended again. We looked to the door. It remained a door—closed.

Paul filled the void again. "I'm sorry, man."

"Sorry?"

Paul grinned. "Sorry that I'm going to fuck your wife so thoroughly she's not going to be able to walk straight for a week."

Beth, appearing in the doorway, got her question out first. "Is that so?"

She'd stripped out of her jeans and sweater, adding a pair of black thigh highs and my favorite pair of heels to her bra and thong combo.

"Paul, what did I tell you this morning about egos getting in the way?"

She stepped in and Casey followed. The diminutive brunette's lingerie was more understated—a chocolate brown pair of boyshorts and a matching bra—but on a body as compact, yet as curvy as hers, it looked great. What was really startling was that her glasses were gone—contacts, maybe—and all hint of the nerdy girl I always knew was wiped away by this beauty.

Amber completed their entrance that felt more like the beginning of a Victoria's Secret fashion show than that of friends. I recognized the pink set as Beth's: the thong, the garter belt clipped into lacy, nude-colored stockings, the lightly padded bra. It had never looked like this on my wife, though, particularly the way Amber's tits spilled over the cups.

I looked at Paul long enough to communicate a *see, told you this was going to be good.*

Beth took a seat on the end of the bed, leaning back onto her arms. She looked up at Amber, who smiled back.

Without looking away from her, Beth said, "So here's what I heard, Jason. Your biggest fantasy is to watch me and Amber hook up?"

My heart skipped a beat. She'd heard?

"That would be really hot," I said.

Amber raked her fingers through her loose locks. She lowered herself to her knees as she spoke. Her smile never faded. "I don't know, Jason. I don't really do girls."

Beth added, "And what would that do to our friendship?"

Beth lifted her hips as Amber took hold of her panties and peeled them off. She shot a quick look at me, winking as she spread her legs open for her best friend.

Amber traced Beth's landing strip with her thumb, leaning forward. "I guess we'll have to risk it."

She leaned forward, her lips finding Beth's as she pushed her fingers into Beth's pussy. Beth broke the kiss with a moan. Amber kissed her neck, reaching behind my wife to remove her bra. Then she went to work on her tits.

"Pretty sexy, huh?" Casey's question came hot against my ear. She was right beside me, leaning over and offering the deep expanse of her cleavage. "Let's make it sexier. Keep watching them."

I did as I was told. As Amber kissed down Beth's naked body, Casey lowered herself between my legs and worked my zipper open.

Beth rolled her head to the side, giving me a lazy smile. "We thought we could improve on your fantasy."

Casey enveloped my cock just as Amber's mouth touched down on her pussy. I gripped the arm of the chair, fighting the sudden, intense desire to come.

"Oh, God, Amb. Yes!" Listening to my wife's voice shake as another woman went down on her didn't ease that desire.

Amber kept working her middle and fore fingers inside Beth, twisting them in and out as she lashed her tongue across Beth's clit. The wet sounds of oral sex roared in my ears. I burned the visual into my brain.

Beth's body crunched inward as she stuttered closer to orgasm. Her face tightened. Her mouth yawned in a silent gasp.

Amber added a third finger, and Beth's gasp was no longer silent. She careened through another shaky moan, flopping back on the bed. Chest thrust out, she wrapped her legs around Amber's head and back and came hard and loud—a sound so familiar to me, yet so strange to hear remotely. I realized that while I'd watched her in action last night, I never saw her *come*. Not with someone else.

Beth's cries in my ears and Casey's mouth on my cock overwhelmed me. I was caught off guard by the swift ferocity of my own orgasm. I came like a teenager getting his first blowjob, joining my wife in the final throes of her release.

Casey swallowed everything, keeping me in her mouth until I was too sensitive to take it. "No more," I begged off, pushing her back.

She wiped her mouth on the back of her hand and smiled. "That was fun."

"Thank you."

On the bed, Amber crawled up Beth's heaving body, dribbling kisses as she went.

"You're so hot, Beth baby," Amber said as she sucked on Beth's hard nipples. The women kissed, full of passion. This wasn't a show. This was an expression of pure, unadulterated lust.

When Amber pulled out of the kiss, Beth looked over at me. "Fantasy come true?"

"Oh, yeah. Looked like you had a good time, too."

Beth smiled without answering and turned to the other man strapped to a chair. "And how about you, Paul? Enjoying the show?"

"You two are damn fine. I can't believe you just did that, Amber."

The blonde blushed. She and Beth sat up, still in one another's arms, their fingers absently caressing one another.

Amber answered Paul, but looked at Beth the whole time. "If I'm honest, I've probably wanted to do that for a while."

The women kissed again. Amber's bra came off. Beth dipped her lips down to nuzzle Amber's neck. "Me, too."

Paul cleared his throat. "You know...I'm feeling a little lonely over here..."

"Oh, poor baby," Amber said. She crawled off the bed and took a seat in Paul's lap. "Feeling neglected? Envious, maybe, that Jason got off and you didn't? Want me to untie you?"

"Please."

Casey went to the nightstand and retrieved something, but I was too focused on Amber and Paul to see what it is.

She went to her knees, freeing Paul's legs. "That better?"

"Now my arms."

"Not so fast. First…" Her grin was pure evil. Unbuckling his belt, she whipped it off and tossed it into the corner. "If I freed your arms, then you might get some ideas in your head, and we wouldn't want that."

She yanked his pants down, taking his boxers with them. His cock sprang free, healthy and hard.

"Instead, you're going to just sit there and watch as Beth, Casey, and I have amazing, lesbian sex. You don't even get a hand to jerk off with."

On cue, Beth's moan drew our attention back to the bed. She was on her back again, legs open as Casey tickled her glass dildo along her pussy. "Ooo, that's nice, Case."

"You know, I've never used one of these before." Casey angled the glass head against Beth and dipped it inside. Beth's breath caught. "Think I should get one?"

"Glass?" Beth asked, her voice tight. "I just got this one but…but yeah, it's pretty…uhhh…pretty awesome."

Amber stood, kissed Paul, and joined the two on the bed. She went right for my wife's lips, kissing her on the mouth. "Ready to return the favor?"

"Mmm, please."

Amber swung her leg over Beth's head, lowering her panty clad pussy. Beth eased the pink thong to the side and raised her mouth to her best friend's sex.

A lesbian threesome and my Beth was right in the middle of it. I was up again, hard and ready for more action.

Instead, all I could do was watch—which for a guy nicknamed Mr. Voyeur wasn't entirely a bad thing.

The women made love like art come alive. Their smooth, elegant bodies complimented one another as they shifted and writhed. Amber leaned down, meeting Casey for a kiss before completing the sixty-nine with Beth. Casey didn't relent with the glassy dildo, driving it into Beth in time with Amber's licks.

Beth dropped her head to the mattress, lips glistening with Amber's juices, nostrils flaring. I knew that look; she was riding the precipice of her orgasm. I'd seen it so many times before—the tightness around her eyes, the concentration gathered in her face—just never when she was with someone else.

I struggled with the restraints, but they held secure. I wanted to join her. Be with her. Kiss her mouth as Casey and Amber rocked her world.

Instead, I watched.

Her moans came deep and heavy. She gripped the sheets. Amber's tongue flicked and flapped across her clit. Casey dipped the dildo in again and again, angling the rigid grooves across her g-spot.

"Oh...oh—fuck me!" Beth's body tightened, surging off the bed. Casey shifted, and Beth's body seized. "What are you—AH!"

The glass dildo was still lodged inside Beth's pussy, but Casey's tongue had drifted lower. My eyes shot wide. She was tonguing Beth's anus.

"Oh—fuck! Ohfuck!" Beth went crazy, writhing at the unfamiliar sensation. Her hips came off the mattress, her legs hooked over Casey's shoulders.

"You like that?" Amber asked, an edge of dominance in her voice that hadn't been there a moment ago. "You naughty slut you, liking your ass licked."

Amber shifted off of Beth, pulling a bottle of lube from the nightstand and handing it to Casey.

"We're just getting you ready for your ultimate fantasy, sweetheart. And I think these two gentlemen are nearly ready, too."

Casey eased the dildo out of Beth's cunt and smeared the lube up and down its glassy surface. I knew what came next, yet wasn't going to believe it until I saw it. "Just relax," she told Beth as she set the tip against Beth's asshole. "You've done this before, right?"

"Mmm hmm…" Beth groaned as Casey applied pressure to the dildo. "But fuck, that feels huge."

"Shh, shh. Relax, Beth. Relax…"

Slowly, the glass sank into my wife's butt. Beth gasped at each ridge, her asshole getting used to the fake cock as it grew wider at the base, writhing up and away. Casey didn't let her get too far, holding her hips down as she drove it in, slowly but firmly.

Amber appeared before me, blocking my view of Beth's anal probing. She'd stripped out of her bra and thong, leaving on her garter belt and stockings to frame her clean shaven mound. "Ready for your wife to get thoroughly, relentlessly fucked?"

I didn't know how to answer that, other than to nod. Amber laughed. "Why don't I check?"

She turned, presenting her glorious ass to me, and sat down in my lap. Deftly, she positioned my cock against her pussy and enveloped me.

Amber moaned. "Mmm, yeah. That feels nice and hard." She looked across the bed at her husband, who was now watching the two of us, not the sight on the bed. "You like how that looks, Pauly? You like Jason's cock stretching me out?"

Paul just grunted, but his erection twitched lewdly in his lap as he did.

Amber went on, relentless. "I'm not sure I'm going to be able to give this up, Paul. Maybe I'll need to come out here to get my fill, if Beth'll let me."

"God, that's so hot." Beth moaned. She was also watching me and Amber, her eyelids heavy with desire. "Come over whenever you want, Amb. You know you're always welcome."

I was barely part of this equation, even though I was the one getting fucked. I was the object: the conversation was all about Amber, Paul, and Beth.

Amber reached between us, fondling her clit as she rode me. "Or maybe I'll just have to find my own boy-toy to play with."

Paul pulled at his restraints, but they held secure. He settled on grinding his teeth.

"Next time I meet a guy like Andrew, I'm not going to turn him down. I'm going to let him wine me, dine me, and then take me back to his place and let him have his way with me. How do you like the sound of that?"

"You're such a slut."

"You wouldn't want it any other way, baby." She looked at the bed, where Casey had found a rhythm fucking Beth's ass and tonguing her clit. "But seriously, Beth's the slut here. She's the one having anal sex."

I gasped, coming so close to losing it. Amber twisted around, kissing me on the mouth. "Feels like you're physically ready, but now it's your turn to squirm."

She stood, leaving me wet and exposed, and crossed around the bed, trailing her hand along Casey's backside. Paul grinned as she approached, knowing he was about to be given his freedom.

Amber knelt down next to him, going to work on the ties around his wrists. "You've been such a good boy, but I want to be honest with you, baby. Last night, when Jason fucked me, he reminded me of what a real man can do with a cock."

I saw Paul's jaw tighten at the taunt. Amber freed his arm, and immediately he grabbed her by her long, blonde mane. I tensed, worried that she'd pushed him too far. Amber cried out, but it wasn't one of pain or fear.

"Maybe I need to remind you of what nine inches can feel like."

"I have a better idea. Why don't you show Beth?"

Paul stripped out of his clothes like a man possessed. I'd never seen a bull paw the ground and charge but I got the feeling it probably looked a hell of a lot like this. I'm not into guys, but even I had to admit that naked, Paul was one hell of a male specimen. Broad shoulders, thick arms, toned upper body, and an actual six-pack—the guy was the perfect match for a chick as hot as Amber, which made him intimidating now that I thought about him with Beth.

But I had nothing to worry about.

Casey cleared out, taking the dildo with her. Beth had only a moment to come to her senses before Paul was upon her, his monster dick splitting her primed pussy.

I jerked in my chair like I'd been punched. Like I'd been fucking body slammed. My Beth with her long limbs and dark hair, splayed out and skewered by my best friend. He lifted her legs over his shoulders and folded her in half as he rammed all nine-inches into her depths.

If I hadn't come earlier, I would have erupted. No touching needed. I almost did even with the buffer. It was the single, most visceral sensation I'd ever felt in my life. I'd never been so jealous and turned on all at the same moment, and the sensations smothered me alive.

"Oh! FUCK!" Beth screamed. My Beth. Screaming. For another man.

He power fucked her, taking her harder than I ever felt comfortable—taking her like I wasn't sure I was capable of. Based on the way she met his thrusts, the way she tossed her head back and forth and cried on the end of his cock, she loved it.

Amber and Casey were at my side, untying the restraints holding me down. "You'll get your chance soon," Amber whispered, once again playing instigator. "For now, just enjoy the show."

Free from my ties, I stayed put as I was told. Casey took Amber's hand and led the blonde to the other chair, where the two settled in beside one another, caressing each other's bodies as they watched the torrid action on the bed.

Beth came hard, her orgasm spilling into the next as her scream shattered my ear drums. Paul finally slowed his onslaught, although he wasn't through with her. Relaxing her legs to either side, he leaned down and kissed her hotly on the mouth.

More than anything else I'd seen, it was that kiss that felt most like a betrayal. When she broke free, Beth looked in my direction, sensing my anxiety. Our eyes met. She seemed to say, *Get your ass over here.*

Finally, it was my turn to join. I stood, shucking my shirt off and kicking out of my pants. Paul may have looked like a male model, but I wasn't a slouch myself.

Beth rolled Paul over, keeping his cock lodged inside her while gracefully taking a spot straddling him. I grabbed the lube, sitting forgotten at the edge of the bed, and squeezed a healthy amount along my length.

Was I really about to do this? Was I really about to violate Beth's ass as another man filled her pussy? I watched Beth rise and fall on Paul's cock, her knees tucked up on either side of him, her ass round and tempting.

Was I going to do this? Fuck yeah I was.

I climbed onto the bed behind Beth. My cock felt like a steel pipe in my hand.

She felt me behind her, sinking down until Paul was ball-deep in her and her ass was still. Reaching behind, she spread her cheeks open for me. She watched me out of the corner of her eyes, part fear, part excitement. They were all watching me, holding their breaths as

I edged closer to her asshole.

Casey's preparation made it easier, but her ass was still as tight as I remembered from years ago, when we'd tried this before. If anything, with Paul lodged in her other hole, she was even tighter.

When my head popped past her vice-like opening, she cried out so sharply that I nearly pulled back out.

Beth's breaths were a shallow staccato. I froze, letting her get used to the sensation. Her moans coalesced into a word—a thought—a strained cry: *oh my God!*

I worked her with short pumps, slow yet persistent. Each forward thrust pushed me a little deeper into her ass, the ring of pressure an agony of pleasure as it worked down my length. Beth was one long groan, punctuated only by quick gasps and fervent cries for god and for being so full.

I balanced myself on her back, clammy and hot from all the sex. When I finally buried myself to the root, my pubic hair brushed up against those smooth cheeks, Beth could barely breathe.

"So...full..." She buried her face in Paul's shoulder as she got used to two men at once. "I feel so...fucking full!"

Then we began to fuck her. We took it slow at first, getting used to our own limits. I could feel Paul move inside her, stretching her even as I fucked her ass. It was a strange feeling—raunchy by every stretch of the imagination—yet so completely sexy.

"That's so hot," Amber whispered to my right. She was still snuggled on the chair with Casey, although they were now fingering one another as they watched. "How do you feel, Beth?"

"Jesus Christ! Uhh!"

Casey giggled. "That sounds about right."

"Fuck me. Ooh, fuck me, you two. Fuck my pussy. Fuck my ass. Oh my God. Oh my God!"

I took control of her hips as Paul and I established an upbeat rhythm, working her in turns—a cock always buried deep. She never had a moment to rest. To relax. To catch her breath and move on. We fucked her until her cries smeared together into one non-stop orgasm.

Amber and Casey closed in on their own orgasms. I chanced a look, catching their fingers fluttering over the other's pussies as they watched. Casey writhed at Amber's touch, the first of our group to lose it.

Beth's ass clamped down on my cock, forcing me back to the debauchery of our MFM threesome. I lasted two strokes—two tight, arduous strokes—and I was there.

"God, Beth, I'm—"

"Oh, Jace! Come, baby. Come!"

I rammed home one last time, digging my thumbs into her ass cheeks as I erupted. Somewhere in the distance, I felt Paul join us, but everything was too clouded in my heady orgasm to tell. I came and came, shoving myself against her buttocks, milking my balls between our heaving bodies.

Beth screamed, guttural and torn. Screamed at being full. Screamed at being filled. Screamed about how good it felt to be taken.

I collapsed onto her back, sandwiching her between me and Paul. The haziness grew. Exhaustion descended. I rolled off her, staring at the ceiling. Beth snuggled in between us, gulping for air. She released a very satisfied sigh.

"That was...amazing." Her voice was hoarse.

"You were incredible," Paul agreed.

"I'm going to be sore for a month!"

I traced down her arm, found her hand, and entwined my fingers with hers. "Me too, and I didn't come close to what you just did."

"Thank you, Jason."

"Thank me?" I chuckled, but it came out more as a sigh. "After everything that's gone down this weekend, we could be thanking each other until we're dead."

"So that's everyone, right?" Beth asked. "No one's got a fantasy they haven't fulfilled?"

Casey climbed out of her chair and started going around the room, blowing out the candles that hadn't burned out. She said, "After watching you just now, I've got a few new fantasies."

Beth laughed.

"Me too," Amber agreed. "And to be fair, my fantasy involved a one-night-stand. This is night two."

Beth laughed. "You didn't need to fuck my husband again tonight."

"Nothing about this weekend was about need. It was about want. And I so wanted to fuck him again."

"I'm glad you did," Beth said.

"Me too," admitted Paul.

The room grew darker and darker as Casey moved through the room, her naked body becoming a shadow. The thought of doing her again—literally the girl-next-door for so many years of my life—was a huge turn-on. But even that couldn't get me to stir.

I was done for the night. We were all done. The candles weren't the only things that had burned down to stubs.

Casey didn't climb back into our crowded bed when she'd finished her task. She took a seat on my side, leaned over, and kissed me softly on the cheek.

"You married a winner, Jason. Don't fuck it up."

With a smile to Beth, Casey glided to the door. She stopped just inside the doorframe, posing like a pinup. There was just enough light seeping in from the snowy outdoors to illuminate her curves. She almost seemed to be saying: *look at this ass, it could be yours one day.*

Looking over her shoulder, Casey said, "Hey, Amb, my invitation is always open. You're always welcome in Philly, and Adam would love to get to know you. Tall, blonde and feisty...I happen to know from experience that you're just his type."

With that, Casey slipped into the hall.

"Her invitation?" Paul asked when she was gone.

"Yeah. Case offered to lend her boyfriend to me. They've got a pretty open relationship."

"Don't I get a say in this?" Paul protested.

"Of course, honey, but I don't think you actually want one, do you?" Amber slipped out of bed. "Come on, let's take this discussion to our room and leave the Old Marrieds alone."

Paul followed her out, although not before looking back at us and grinning. "I'm going to marry her."

And then Beth and I were alone for what felt like the first time in a year. Beth snuggled against me and asked the question that was also on my mind. "Are we good?"

I didn't want to give her an immediate, canned answer. I gathered my thoughts, going over all that had gone down this weekend. We'd had sex in front of another couple, then swapped partners. I'd had a threesome with two women—as did Amber. Beth had sex with her best friend and Maid of Honor. And then she had sex with two guys at the same time.

My wife—my Beth—had done all that.

"I'd be lying if I said I'm not in total shock, but yeah, I'd say we're pretty good." I said it with a mirth that wasn't put on or forced. This was a conversation too bizarre to believe. "How are you feeling, honey?"

"Sore." She laughed. "But really...satisfied—and not in the way you're thinking, although it's that, too. You know that feeling you get when you watch people open the presents you gave them on Christmas?"

"Yeah. It's a good feeling."

"And it's even better when you know you really nailed it, right? Like you found the perfect gift, and watch their eyes light up as they unwrap. I feel like I just gave all of our friends—and you, baby—perfect gifts. And it was fucking awesome to watch."

"What about you? Was it as fun to receive as it was to give?"

Beth hugged me tight, her voice growing husky. "What do you think?"

"So is this going to be, like, a thing?"

"Don't overthink it. As long as I have you and you have me—and we always keep the two of us at the heart of everything—then I could care less what it is, or what society would classify it as." She pulled the sheets over us now that the room had begun to cool down. "But I have a feeling that we just got a lot closer to Paul and Amber."

"You think they're going to be okay?"

"Paul and Amber? I think so. They're good for each other, even when they're butting heads. She needs someone like him: someone she can't push over."

"Can't push over all the time," I corrected.

"True statement."

I added, "And Paul needs a woman like Amber who will challenge him. Otherwise, he'll get bored."

"Something tells me she's not going to get boring any time soon."

We shared a laugh.

"So you're totally cool with this weekend?" I asked as sleep started to pull us away.

"You mean, am I cool knowing I have a husband who can keep up with three sexed up females and *still* perform like you just did?"

I smiled. How could I not? "Not exactly where I was going. I mean, you know, were you jealous? Or...I don't know...have any regrets?"

"Those are two very different questions. Did I get jealous? Of course. You did, too. Do I regret what we did? No way. The only reason I would is if I thought we'd damaged something between us. I think we not only learned a few things about each other, but that we're actually stronger because of it."

"You sure you're not just rationalizing an orgy-filled weekend?" I said.

Beth laughed. "To be fair, we only had one orgy."

"Last night by the fire seemed like one."

"Okay, orgy expert. But I don't think I'm just rationalizing. Do you?"

"No. I'm just teasing." I touched her hair, finding her face in the dark. "I love that I'm still learning things about you. Makes me excited about the rest of our lives together."

Beth giggled. "It's not all going to be like this, you know."

"Good, because I don't think my body could keep up."

"Then I won't tell you that what I've always wanted was actually three guys, all at the same time."

"Oh, Jesus." My cock stirred at last.

"Good night, Jason. Sweet dreams."

"Night, Beth. I love you."

Epilogue

Paul and Amber left after breakfast the next day. We finished digging out the driveway, but it was already warming up. In two days, most of the snow would be gone. Such was the reality of the Maryland suburbs, despite what the local news channels said.

We didn't have another orgy that morning, and our goodbyes weren't laden with gropes and French kisses. They were the same goodbyes that we'd always shared: close, intimate, casual, and most importantly, without awkwardness.

I drove Casey to the train station once it was clear that the trains were running again. The world had started to crawl out from under the snow, but it was still pretty empty.

"So you and your boyfriend do this kind of thing all the time?" I asked when we hit a desolate highway.

"Have orgy-fueled birthday weekends? Not at all."

"Maybe not a birthday weekend then..."

I chanced a glance at Casey, who with smiling out the window. Her glasses were back in place, and her hair was tied back, giving her the nerdy librarian look I remembered from high school.

"You've got the wrong impression about us. About me. I'm still the girl you grew up with."

"You still play World of Warcraft?"

Casey laughed. "Actually, sometimes, but casually now. But that's not what I'm talking about."

"You mean how you're guarded. How you don't let anyone in. How you only had two other close friends, me and Paul, and only because we were all neighbors?"

"Something like that, yeah," she said. "It's been a long time since I've met someone I could trust, like I can you and Paul."

"And this guy...?"

"I can trust. And that opens up so many fun possibilities."

"I see."

"You and Beth have it, too. In fact, it's the two of you who made me realize that I even *wanted* to open up. I was so guarded, so careful. Then I watched her walk down the aisle—watched the way you looked at each other—and I realized that I wanted that."

"Yeah, I'm a pretty lucky guy."

"You are. And something tells me you two are going to have a lot of fun over the years. Just keep talking—all the time, always communicating. And don't be afraid to be a little naughty. Trust, remember?"

"Didn't I give you this advice yesterday?"

Casey laughed. "Maybe." We pulled into the train station's lot. "I made a video to share with him. Want to see?"

"From last night?" My heart skipped a beat.

"Yeah." She held up her phone. "After you guys went to bed, I joined Amber and Paul. There was one more combo we hadn't tried."

Casey was on the screen, on her hands and knees. Paul was positioned behind her.

She hit play, and the image came alive.

Yes! Yes! Fuck me with that giant cock!

Paul slapped her ass, taking her with the same ferocity I'd watched her take Beth. He reached down, grabbed Casey by her loose mane of hair, and yanked her head back.

You like that? You like it rough?!

Casey answered with a spill of moans, an elongated *fuuuuck* that ended in a scream that I can't believe I'd slept through last night.

Casey hit pause and the scene stopped. "That was fun."

"And your boyfriend is okay with that?"

Casey cracked a smile. "My boyfriend spent his weekend snowed in with our boss, fucking her brains out."

"I see." I had to laugh. "You know you're welcome to stay longer."

"I bet you'd like that, wouldn't you?" She winked. "But I'd like to get home, you know?"

"To meet up with your boyfriend and...boss?"

Casey shook her head. "Just him."

She didn't need to say that she missed her boyfriend for me to hear it.

She hugged me across the gear shift. "Thanks for inviting me down. And happy birthday, Jason."

"You're always welcome."

"I know. Thanks. But next time you decide to throw a wild, orgy-filled sex party, let me know ahead of time. I'll make sure to bring a date."

"Will do. I'd like to meet this guy, Adam, sometime."

"Oh, you will. Don't worry. I think you two would get along. And I think you and Beth owe him a few experiences..."

"Bye, Casey. It was really good to see you."

"You two, Jason. You too."

And that was our snowed in weekend. A weekend of fantasy fulfillment and adventure. Beth and I relived it in the weeks and months that followed, although we didn't repeat it with Amber and Paul.

Not at first, anyway. Not until Paul proposed to Amber and Beth arranged a bachelorette party in Vegas.

But that's a totally different story.

Acknowledgements

This book, like everything that eventually comes to market from me, has been a long time in coming. It's evolved over the years since it's first inception—inspired, naturally, by a blizzard a few years ago that buried me and my wife at home. Too bad we didn't have friends like Casey, Paul, and Amber to spend it with, but it was a good time, nonetheless. I hope you enjoyed the end result; I certainly enjoyed writing it.

And yes, that was Casey from *Unconventional*. Haven't read *Unconventional*? If you want more of Casey, check it out. If you want even more, drop me an email: kennywright.writer@gmail.com.

Couldn't have done any of it without these amazing folks:

Lucy V. Morgan, who not only edited this bad boy, but helped me with my cover when I was coming up blank, she's a great advisor, image searcher, and best of all, friend;

Stephen, my more-than-a-beta-reader beta reader...also, tax advisor and all around great guy;

The good folks who've helped me found eroticaformen.com (check out the new site if you're looking for more quality erotica: Kirsten McCurran, Max Sebastian, and Ben Boswell;

My wife, my wife, forever my wife.

And all of you for buying the book. I say it every time, and every time I mean it more. If I believed in being blessed, I'd say I'm blessed. Instead, I'll just say I'm lucky to have you. If you liked it, leave a review, tell a friend, or tell me if you want I love hearing about it.

Stay warm!

About the Author

I'm just a guy who writes what I like to read: steamy, explicit erotica that's just crazy enough to be true. I write romantic erotica. I write about characters that I like, and endings that feel natural. I write stories where husbands watch their wives get naughty. I write about MILFs and erotic games and loss of innocence. I believe in a world where men read and appreciate erotica, and hope to contribute to it word by word.

Find me online at www.kennywriter.com, or follow me on Twitter at @kennywriter.

Also by Kenny Wright

After School Special (A Short)
All In: Strip Poker Done Right
Because He's Watching; Ian's Obsession
Eight Hundred Dollar Heels (A Short)
Just Watch Me
Leap
Moving Mrs. Mitchell (A Short)
Naughty But Nice (A Short)
Rediscovering Danielle (A Short)
Something Forbidden
Unconventional: Business or Pleasure
While She Watches

For a full list of titles, along with their covers, synopses, and where to purchase, go to www.kennywriter.com/books.